There was a small smile on Ry's handsome face as he looked into her eyes in the light of the street lamp.

But just when Kate expected more cajoling and coaxing, that wasn't what he did.

What he did was lean over the door to press his mouth to hers. Only for a moment. Stealing a kiss instead.

And then it was over so quickly she hadn't even had a chance to react or kiss him back—not that she'd wanted to.

"I thought I wasn't your type?" she said, raising her chin to him as if that slight buss hadn't added to the earlier touch of his hand to make her knees go just a little wobbly.

"Yeah...I keep telling myself that," he said in an almost-whisper.

Dear Reader,

Kate Perry has a goal—to get married and have kids. But she's wasted a lot of time with immature men who have strung her along. So now she has a plan—she's joined dating services and will agree to meet only men who list their own goal as marriage and family, men who give no indication of immaturity in any form.

Then in swoops Ry Grayson, flying his own plane, his shoulder injured in a skateboarding mishap, already touted as a daredevil kid-at-heart. So he instantly doesn't make the cut.

Of course, the conservative, small-town reverend's granddaughter isn't Ry's type, either. He just needs her help solving the mystery of his grandmother's past. The problem is, sometimes being together reveals that there's more than meets the eye....

Welcome back to Northbridge. I hope it feels like home to you.

Always the best,

Victoria Pade

THE BACHELOR'S NORTHBRIDGE BRIDE

VICTORIA PADE

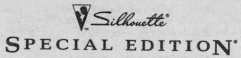

Silhouette®

SPECIAL EDITION®

Published by Silhouette Books

America's Publisher of Contemporary Romance

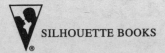

SILHOUETTE BOOKS

ISBN-13: 978-0-373-65502-1

Recycling programs
for this product may
not exist in your area.

THE BACHELOR'S NORTHBRIDGE BRIDE

Visit Silhouette Books at www.eHarlequin.com

Printed in U.S.A.

Books by Victoria Pade

VICTORIA PADE

is a *USA TODAY* bestselling author of numerous romance novels. She has two beautiful and talented daughters—Cori and Erin—and is a native of Colorado, where she lives and writes. A devoted chocolate lover, she's in search of the perfect chocolate chip cookie recipe. For information about her latest and upcoming releases, and to find recipes for some of the decadent desserts her characters enjoy, log on to www.vikkipade.com.

Chapter One

"Here he comes!"

Kate Perry heard the announcement of the excited bride just as Kate ducked in reflex to the sound of a plane flying so low overhead that she thought it was going to crash into the Graysons' house.

Kate watched her soon-to-be-sister-in-law rush through the French doors that opened onto the balcony outside the second-floor bedroom. From there Marti Grayson waved wildly as two of the other bridesmaids followed behind. Kate only reluctantly brought up the rear. She wasn't sure she wanted to be on the balcony of the decaying old house if the plane made a second pass.

Which it did just as she got outside, towing a banner that said *CONGRATULATIONS MARTI AND NOAH*.

"That's Ry," Marti said with a laugh, enjoying the spectacle as the plane flew off this time.

Marti Grayson was about to marry Kate's brother Noah. Kate and her sister Meg were two of the four bridesmaids, but Meg was helping Noah with his tie while Kate stayed with the bride and the other bridesmaids.

But Kate seemed to be the only one of the group who had found it alarming to have a plane take a dive toward the house.

"I know Noah said your brother was flying in but did that mean he pilots his own plane?" she asked, wondering if she'd missed that bit of information somewhere along the line.

"That's what it means," Marti confirmed. "You name it, Ry does it—flies his own plane, races cars and motorcycles, does extreme sports, dives off cliffs—he'll do anything. He has no fear, our Ry. He's just a great big kid at heart. I don't think he'll ever grow up," the bride concluded affectionately.

Kate forced a smile at her soon-to-be-sister-in-law's amusement. But to Kate, what Marti was saying about Ry Grayson—and many of the other things Kate had heard about him—just made him sound reckless and immature.

She kept her opinion to herself, though, as everyone moved back into the bedroom to continue the last-minute wedding preparations. Her preliminary opinion of Ry Grayson wasn't important to anyone but her.

"I can't wait for Ry to meet you, Kate," Marti was saying. "I know you were out of town for Wyatt and Neily's wedding a few weeks ago so you didn't get to meet him then, but you're going to love him—everybody does."

Kate did the smile again, adding a nod this time.

She knew everyone who had met the third Grayson triplet when he'd been in her small hometown of Northbridge, Montana, had liked him. And was still talking about him even though three weeks had gone by. *Full of life. Will do anything for a good time. Over-the-top crazy man. Fun, fun, fun...*

Those were only some of the things Kate had heard said of Ry Grayson. And swooping around in a plane with a congratulations banner? That was going to win him more popularity points with everyone else.

The Grayson triplets were the grandchildren of Theresa Hobbs Grayson, a native of Northbridge who had left town over fifty years ago. Theresa had only recently returned in the midst of a particularly bad episode of the mental instability and dementia she suffered. It had brought her back to her deserted family home in search of something she claimed to have had taken from her.

Her grandchildren, Marti, Wyatt and Ry—who were also her guardians—had opted to let Theresa remain in Northbridge while they sorted through her history and tried to make right the wrongs Theresa believed were done to her long ago.

In Northbridge, both Wyatt and Marti had made lovematches—Wyatt with Neily Pratt, and now Marti with Kate's brother Noah. But while Kate liked the down-toearth Wyatt and Marti, she wasn't looking forward to meeting the more showy Ry.

There was a knock on the bedroom door just then and Kate's sister Meg came in carrying a box full of tiny white daisies.

"The florist said these are for everyone's hair," Meg said as she set the box on the bed.

"They're a surprise!" Marti informed them. "I asked for these with you in mind, Kate. They seemed like the perfect thing for that curly red hair and the way you're wearing it pulled back today. So everyone gets them since we didn't plan headpieces or hats."

Kate appreciated the special thought and took her share of the daisies to one of several mirrors set around the room for the occasion.

Curly red hair—that was what she had all right. Not wiry, coarse curls, just big waves of thick hair the color of red mahogany.

It was good hair. In fact, in high school, it had been voted Best Hair. But Kate sometimes wondered if it got her into trouble. If maybe the novelty of it drew the attention of the sort of men she was now dead set against getting involved with again.

Maybe she should dye it.

Change her hair color, maybe change her luck with men? It was a thought....

Careful attention was required for Kate to intersperse the flowers among the curls but even so, she was the first to finish while Meg and the other two bridesmaids continued to place them as artfully as possible in their own hairdos.

She asked if anyone wanted help but since they didn't, she used the time to make a final assessment of the rest of her own appearance.

Mascara brightened her blue-green eyes. Blush helped accentuate her cheekbones in her otherwise pale skin, and she hoped a slight dusting of it across her nose camouflaged what she thought of as a too-narrow and pointy beak.

Her lips were highlighted with a mauve gloss that matched the calf-length, nondescript bridesmaids' dresses. And she loved the earrings that Marti had given her as a gift—they were small teardrop diamonds. Traditional and conservative. Like Kate. Who was just an old-fashioned small-town girl through and through.

Everyone else was still fiddling with the flowers when

a gust of early June wind came through the French doors, left open since the flyby. Kate went to close them and, just as she did, the loud roar of an approaching motorcycle caught her attention from below.

"That will be Ry again," Marti said at the sound. "Wyatt left him a motorcycle in the field where he had to land so he could get here as quick as possible. Now we'll be able to start anytime."

But her brother had only flown overhead about twenty minutes ago. Had he been able to land a plane, hop on a motorcycle and get here already? Apparently all that racing Marti had mentioned paid off.

Kate closed the doors but curiosity kept her there to peer through the glass at the arrival of the helmeted man in coveralls.

Coveralls? They'd at least have to wait for him to change clothes, wouldn't they?

Bounding right up onto the old house's already patchy lawn, the man who was presumably Ry Grayson brought the motorcycle to an abrupt halt, turned off the engine and then sat straddling the big machine with his long legs while he took off his helmet.

Golden-blond sun-streaked hair gleamed in the late Sunday-afternoon sunshine. It was cut short at the sides and in back, but with the removal of the helmet, he ran a big hand through the longer top, managing to muss it to perfection by ruffling his fingers through it.

From the distance Kate couldn't tell the details of his face, but she could see that he was as handsome as she'd heard. He had a sculpted, masculine bone structure and a well-defined, strong chin. There was no doubt in Kate's mind by then that the man was Ry Grayson because he resembled his siblings. And even without close inspection, Kate could tell that Ry was the jewel in the crown when it came to looks. Wyatt and Marti were more than attractive, but Ry was striking.

He hung his helmet on the motorcycle's handlebars and swung a long leg over the seat to get off, standing tall and lean and broad shouldered. Then he yanked apart what must have been snaps holding the coveralls closed and shrugged out of them to reveal a dashingly tailored tuxedo underneath.

First the plane, then the motorcycle and now the stripping off of coveralls to transform into the debonair groomsman—the guy seemed to think he was James Bond.

There was a knock on the bedroom door just then, followed by the photographer asking to take a few shots of the bride and her attendants getting ready.

"Will you let him in, Kate?" Marti asked.

Kate took one last glance at Ry Grayson as he headed for the house, then she tore herself away from the French doors to do the bride's bidding.

But even as she did, she became aware that there was suddenly a tiny flicker of eagerness in her to get this show on the road so she could have a better look at the man who was just coming in downstairs.

But it was a flicker she stomped out the minute she realized it was there.

No more Peter Pans! she swore.

And she meant it.

But why was it that they always seemed to come in such prime packaging? she wondered as she showed the photographer in.

* * *

"Kate! There you are! Finally! Every time I think I'm going to be able to introduce you to Ry you slip away."

Kate smiled at her new sister-in-law as if she didn't know what Marti was talking about when, in fact, Kate had been doing her best to avoid the introduction since the minute the wedding ceremony had ended.

Only now Marti had literally cornered her in the dining room.

"Ry, this is Kate, Noah's other sister—the one you *haven't* met because she couldn't make it to Wyatt's wedding. Kate, this is Ry."

"Kate," he repeated in a deep voice that was so sexy it made just the saying of her name sound like an endearment.

"Nice to meet you," she lied, feeling her smile tighten as she raised her gaze for her first steady, open, straight-on look at Ry Grayson—something else she'd been avoiding.

And was he less handsome when she could scrutinize every detail? Oh, no, it would have been too much to ask for anything about him to have been ordinary. Instead—of course—he was so, so much more handsome close-up than when seen at a distance from the French doors in the bedroom, so much more handsome than she'd been able to see when she'd been averting her eyes.

That prominent chin had a dimple. The corners of his lips quirked up with an intriguing aura of mystery. When he smiled at her, two laugh lines bracketed his mouth like parentheses around a secret he was silently sharing. His nose was exactly the right length and width and straightness. And his eyes weren't merely silver-blue; they were a spectacular, sparkling, metallic silver-blue.

"Where are you in the family order?" he was asking. "Eldest, youngest, somewhere in the middle?"

Kate forced herself to stop counting the ways she could have a weak spot for him if he was a different sort of man and concentrated on his question.

"I'm the youngest but at this time of year, Meg and I are the same age for a while because we're only ten months apart. Jared is the eldest, Noah is second, then Meg and me."

He probably hadn't wanted the details, she chastised herself, he was merely making small talk. It was just that the way he looked in that tuxedo was causing her to be a little scatterbrained.

"I'm the baby of the family, too," he joked. "Wyatt was born first, Marti seven minutes later and me ten minutes after that."

"Does that account for you being the spirit-of-youth in your family?" Kate said then, mostly to remind herself.

His eyebrows dipped together in an amused frown. "The *spirit-of-youth?*"

"The daredevil," she qualified.

"I have been known to take some risks, that's true," he confirmed.

"You nearly scared poor Kate to death when you flew over earlier," Marti contributed in explanation. "I think she thought a plane was about to crash into us."

He hadn't taken his eyes off Kate even when his sister spoke, and he didn't now. "You must be easily frightened," he goaded.

"It *did* sound like you were going to land in the bedroom," Marti said.

He grinned as if that was exactly what he'd been going for. But he finally glanced away from Kate to look at Marti.

"I had to let you know I was on my way," he countered remorselessly. "And I wanted you to see the banner."

Marti rolled her eyes at him, apparently not wanting him to know she'd been delighted by his antics.

But it was to Kate that she said, "I'm forgiving him everything today because he got Gram out of hiding in the kitchen for my wedding—that was where she watched Wyatt's because she's so skittish about being around a lot of people. I don't know if you saw her and Mary Pat, but they came down the stairs and watched from just behind where everyone else was sitting—it made me feel like she was at least a little more a part of it."

"I did see her and her nurse," Kate said. She'd also noticed out of the corner of her eye during the ceremony the frequent glances Ry Grayson had cast in that direction, accompanied by reassuring smiles.

"She'll do things for Ry that none of the rest of us can ever get her to do. He's a master," Marti said with admiration.

"Your grandmother wouldn't stay downstairs afterward, though?" Kate asked because she hadn't seen Theresa since the pronouncement of Noah and Marti as man and wife.

"Not even Ry could get her to do that, no," Marti said sadly. "She's fearful and phobic. And she's particularly embarrassed about facing people in Northbridge—I'm sure Noah has told you that we're just piecing together why that is and trying to convince her that she doesn't need to be."

But as if that wasn't a subject for a festive occasion, Marti changed it and said to her brother, "Ry, I also wanted you to meet Kate because she's a masseuse."

That brought a slow, lascivious smile to Ry Grayson's handsome face. "A masseuse. Really? You know, when someone says *masseuse* the first thing you think of is—"

"Medical massage therapist?" Kate challenged, knowing what he was insinuating.

"Ry…" Marti said in an exaggeratedly reprimanding tone. "You are not honestly making a massage-parlor innuendo to the Reverend's granddaughter—who you just met—at my *wedding,* when I'm trying to get you medical aid, are you?"

"Who? Me?" he asked, the picture of innocence were it not for the gleam of mischief in his remarkable eyes.

Marti shook her head and said to Kate, "He can be incorrigible."

"I never would have guessed," Kate responded partially under her breath.

But rather than being insulted by her remark, Ry Grayson laughed again and his gaze locked onto Kate's once more as if he were enjoying the polite sparring.

"Anyway," Marti continued. "What I was about to tell you, Kate, is that Ry hurt his shoulder yesterday—trying out his neighbor's son's skateboard, if you can believe it. I thought there might be something you could do to help since he couldn't see anyone in Missoula before coming here."

Kate didn't have a chance to respond to that because her own brother appeared behind Marti right then, insisting that there was someone his new bride needed to meet.

"Can I trust you alone with Kate?" Marti asked Ry, rather than merely agreeing to go.

"Absolutely. I'll be on my best behavior," he swore, raising his right hand.

Marti must not have been completely convinced because she still said, "Do *not* give Kate a hard time. Remember she's my sister-in-law now and the *Reverend's* granddaughter."

"Best behavior," Ry repeated.

Marti cast him a warning look before abandoning Kate to him. Kate, who was still backed into a corner.

She raised her chin, wondering if Ry Grayson was going to keep his word to his sister or not, ready for it if he didn't.

Then he surprised her and did.

"So you're Noah's little sister," he said conversationally. "Wyatt and I both think a lot of him."

"I'm glad," Kate said, meaning it.

"We weren't sure anyone could ever replace the guy Marti was with before—Jack. We all knew him since we were little kids and he was more than a friend. He was like one of us. When he was killed in the car accident on the way to their wedding, Wyatt and I grieved almost as much as Marti did."

"It must have been awful," Kate said, her guard dropping a little in spite of herself because what he was saying—confiding—seemed genuine and heartfelt.

"Jack was a hard act to follow," Ry continued. "And even though we never said it to Marti, we didn't think it was possible for us to ever like anyone else as well. But we've talked about it—Wyatt and I—and while Noah is different from Jack, we think he's great."

Okay, so Ry Grayson was gaining ground with every kind word he said about Noah. Kate couldn't help it; she was close to her brothers and sister, they were important to her, and it was nice to know Noah's in-laws were welcoming him so warmly. Nice for Ry Grayson to tell her....

"We feel like we've hit the jackpot with Noah when it comes to the remodel and with the work on the Home-Max location, too," Ry was saying.

Noah was the contractor who had been hired to update and refurbish Theresa Hobbs Grayson's long-neglected childhood home. It was how Noah and Marti had met and from that, Noah had also agreed to do construction on the building that would house the Northbridge branch of the family's chain of home-improvement stores.

Ry went on with his accolades. "There are places in the house where Noah has replaced a section of the original crown molding or the spindles in the staircase and even I can't tell what's new and what's old."

"He is good at what he does," Kate agreed. Then, testing to see just how fond of her brother the Graysons were— and knowing that Noah had been concerned about what Ry and Wyatt Grayson thought about the fact that Marti was pregnant with Noah's baby due to a one-night stand at a hardware convention—she said, "What about the baby? Are you and Wyatt okay with that?"

The question didn't seem to faze Ry. "We're fine with it. Actually…"

He moved slightly toward her as if what he was about to say was even more of a confidence, and Kate caught a whiff of clean, citrusy cologne that was like a breath of fresh orchard air enticing her a fraction of an inch closer to him, too.

"…I hated what Marti had told us before," he said in a slightly quieter voice. "She claimed she'd had artificial insemination and I was afraid she'd done it because she was so lonely after losing Jack that it had driven her to extreme measures. I felt like Wyatt and I must have dropped the ball, that we must not have given her enough time or comfort or attention. That we'd really failed her. But the thought that she had met somebody who made her realize that she hadn't died along with Jack? Somebody she wanted to spend the night with? That just proves she's human and let me know she was getting over Jack's death. And to tell you the truth, it was a relief to me not to have to think we'd let her down somehow."

Kate couldn't help smiling at that. And wishing he hadn't just given her a reason to like him.

"What about your side?" he asked then. "A *reverend's* family? Are you all wanting to hang your heads in shame because the pregnancy came before the wedding? Or thinking less of Marti because of it?"

"No," Kate said without hesitation. "I mean, those of us who know Marti is pregnant don't want to hang our heads in shame and we definitely don't think any less of her."

"Those of you who know?"

"Noah hasn't told the Reverend yet—"

"You call your grandfather *the Reverend?*"

"*No one* calls him anything else," Kate said. Then she went back to answering his question. "The Reverend would be outraged that a member of his family had conceived a child out of wedlock, so Noah put off telling him. In a month or so, Noah will announce it to him as if it's just happened and leave it at that. But the rest of us know, and since this will be our first niece or nephew, we can't wait. Well, *I* can't wait. And Meg is excited, too. We've already started buying baby things. And we really do love Marti. We think of her as another sister. We couldn't have picked anyone better for Noah ourselves."

"No, you couldn't have," Ry Grayson confirmed. Then, with that subject exhausted, he smiled a smile that was reminiscent of his earlier devilish one, and said, "So, we're talking *medical* massage?"

This time there was nothing about his teasing that seemed offensive. "That *is* what I'm trained in, yes," she said. "And you hurt yourself riding a neighbor's kid's *skateboard?*"

He grinned, deepening those lines around his supple mouth. "I suppose it was some of that *spirit-of-youth*," he countered facetiously. "But I've dislocated the shoulder twice before so it doesn't take much to set it off and when I tried the half-pipe I wiped out a few times. As a result the shoulder is pretty stiff and sore. But usually a *therapeutic medical massage* helps."

The way he said that—with a grin—made her smile, too. It was just so dangerous to be enjoying herself with a grown man who had hurt himself skateboarding. Kate knew it as surely as she knew she was standing there. But could she help it? Apparently not, because she *was* enjoying herself.

But just for now, when there was no escape. It wasn't going beyond this.

"I'll be at my office at the hospital in the afternoon tomorrow," she said, forcing a heavy dose of professionalism into her tone. "I'm booked solid but if you come at six, I'll stay an extra hour as a favor to Marti, since you're family," she said, thinking that maybe it might help to put him into those ranks.

"Family…" he repeated. "Hmm…I don't know that I like thinking of my masseuse as *family*."

"That's what we are, though," she insisted. "Just plain old family."

His smile then was small and amused as he shook his head, and his gaze touched on her hair before he said, "I hate to tell you, but there is absolutely nothing about you that's plain."

The hair always did seem to be a factor, she thought, trying to take his flattery with a grain of salt.

Rather than responding to his comment, she said, "It's my turn to take the Reverend home and I'm sure he wants to leave since the cake's been cut. So what'll it be? Six tomorrow night or taking care of it yourself?"

Ry Grayson laughed. Spontaneously, boisterously, wickedly. "Oh, I definitely don't want to take care of it myself. I'll be there at six—I'm sure someone can tell me where the hospital is."

"It's on the west side of Main Street, a block up from South. You could walk from here."

"I'll be there," he assured.

At some point after the lure of Ry's confidences, Kate must have pushed herself against the corner walls again without realizing it because she had to straighten away from them now. But Ry had apparently not backed up any because when she did, it put her much closer to him than she wanted to be. Close enough to smell that cologne again. Too close for comfort.

And he didn't step away and give her any breathing room. He stayed where he was, looking down at her from a full six-foot-three-inch height that towered over her five foot four.

His smile this time was boyish and sexy, and it made Kate's heart beat a bit faster.

"Absolutely *nothing* plain about you," he repeated, more to himself than to her.

Then he pivoted on his heels like a door opening to let her out, and Kate went past him.

"Let me know if you change your mind about tomorrow night so I don't wait around for you," she instructed.

"I need the massage, I won't change my mind."

"I'll see you then, then," she said, feeling dumb for not finding a way to say that without using the word *then* twice.

But once she had moved beyond him, she kept going,

searching for her grandfather so she could get out of there before she had to see Ry Grayson again.

Because while, yes, it was probably good to have established a relatively friendly rapport with her brother's new brother-in-law, that was as far as it would go.

He had a *skateboarding* injury, for crying out loud.

Even without the other things she'd heard about him, even without both of his over-the-top entrances today, what could scream I-don't-want-to-grow-up louder than that?

And not only had she reached a point in her life where she knew exactly what she wanted, she also had experience to teach her what kind of man she could never get it from. Nothing she'd learned about Ry Grayson after meeting him had changed her preliminary opinion of him as that kind of man.

The fact that he was fantastic looking, and as personable and fun loving as all reports had claimed, on top of it?

That just made him a triple threat.

And definitely not a candidate for what she was looking for.

Chapter Two

"So now you're going to be with me for a while, Ry?"

"I am, Gram," Ry confirmed for his grandmother. He didn't point out that it was the third time she'd asked the same question already today and they'd only just finished breakfast. "Marti has gone on her honeymoon and Wyatt went back to Missoula. He'll be here with us one day this week but otherwise, it's just you and me, babe," he joked, making her smile. "Well, you and me and Mary Pat," he amended then.

Theresa's nurse, Mary Pat, suggested she take Theresa to dress for the day. As the two women got up from the table, Theresa said to Ry, "I don't think you're going to like it here."

That was a new one.

Ry raised his eyebrows at her. "Why is that, Gram?"

"It isn't your kind of place. It's quiet, things move more slowly. I don't think it's going to be enough for you."

"You know I can usually stir things up a little," he said, winking at her because he knew it always tickled her.

She waved a hand at him as if she were swatting a fly but giggled anyway before Mary Pat ushered her out of the kitchen.

Ry took a drink of his second cup of coffee.

His grandmother might not always be in her right mind, but there were still some things she had insight into. And despite his making light of it, he thought the possibility that Northbridge wasn't for him was one of those things.

Granted he'd only been here for Wyatt's wedding three weeks ago and again now for Marti's, so he hadn't seen much of Northbridge. And he knew his brother and sister were enamored of the small town. But in spite of the fact that he'd met a lot of nice people, the town itself did seem a little too sleepy for him—too slow and quiet, just like his grandmother had said.

But whether he liked Northbridge or not, he, Wyatt and Marti had always shared the responsibility of their grandmother. When she'd run away from Mary Pat to come here, he and his brother and sister had agreed that if Northbridge was where Theresa wanted to be, Northbridge was where she should be—even if it meant they had to rotate being here with her.

Of course with both Wyatt and Marti married to locals now, there was talk of them relocating permanently. If that happened, Ry thought he could hold down the fort in Missoula where Home-Max was headquartered. Then he wouldn't have to spend much time in Northbridge. But for now, here he was, taking his turn at helping with Theresa.

And not excited by the prospect of being basically sequestered in the Montana outback—as he thought of the small town.

It wasn't that Northbridge was a bad place—from what little he'd seen, it had plenty of charm. But it *was* a small town and any small town had its limitations. And Ry didn't like limitations.

He liked—he thrived on—activity and choices and always having more options for things to do than he had time to do them. Slow and quiet? That was the last thing he wanted.

In fact, he'd meant it when he'd assured Marti and Wyatt before they'd left this morning that he was glad to take over all they'd passed along for him to do. Because even if they had had to pile it on, he would always rather have too much on his plate than not enough.

But he definitely had a full plate for this round.

Along with keeping his grandmother company, there was the new Home-Max they were opening in Northbridge. They'd purchased a series of neighboring storefronts on Main Street that needed some work before they could house the new store, and overseeing the final stages of that was on his to-do list.

He also needed to inventory stock as it was delivered, and organize the beginning of the actual setup of the store.

No question about it, he had more than enough to keep him busy with all of that.

And there was also this Hector Tyson guy he had to look up, the guy who had taken unfair advantage of the young Theresa and who now had a lot to answer for, a lot Ry was determined to make him answer for.

Plus, along those same lines, there was the mystery from his grandmother's past that he and his siblings were trying to solve once and for all—he'd promised to get into that, too, to try to figure out what exactly it was that his grandmother claimed had been taken from her, what exactly it was that she'd come to Northbridge to reclaim. If it might be more than the land Tyson had done her out of. If it might actually be a lost child...

And of course there was his massage tonight....

From Kate Perry.

There hadn't been any shortage of thoughts about her to occupy him since he'd first set eyes on her yesterday. Even though he wished they would stop coming.

But damn, what a beauty she was! He'd already known that Northbridge had more than its fair share of pretty women from the abundance of them at Wyatt's wedding. But Kate Perry? He'd hardly been able to believe his eyes when he'd gotten his first glimpse of her. And even though she'd been coming down the aisle between two sections of folding chairs in his grandmother's old house, his first thought was that she could have been a vision emerging from a mist on an Irish countryside.

Not that he had any idea if she was even Irish. It was just her coloring that made him think Irish lass—that incredible, lush, thick red hair and that pale alabaster skin. Add to it the delicate lines of her nose and apple-colored cheeks, and the pure elegance of her jaw, and she looked more like she was made of porcelain than skin and bone.

Then her compact, posture-perfect, curves-in-all-the-right-places self had reached the makeshift altar where the ceremony was to be held. And in casting her eyes back the way she'd come to watch for the remainder of the bridesmaids and the bride, they'd briefly touched on him where he'd stood with Noah and some of the other groomsmen across the aisle.

But the glance had been just long enough for him to see

that her eyes weren't merely blue, they weren't merely green; they were a perfect combination of the two—like the mingling of sea and sky. Bright, vibrant, almost electric—they were amazing eyes to complete the picture of a truly, amazingly beautiful woman.

Just the memory was enough to take his breath away a little.

One look at her at that moment and everything else— every other person in the room—including his sister walking down the aisle—every sound, every note of the music being played, every scent of perfume and flowers, *everything* had faded into a blur as the only clear image he'd had, the only thing he'd been aware of, was Kate Perry.

It was the weirdest thing that had ever happened to him.

Of course he'd shaken it off and poured his concentration back into the wedding. But as he sat there at the breakfast table Monday morning, taking another drink of his coffee, he still couldn't help thinking about it, thinking about her. And how it was slightly unnerving to have had such a powerful first reaction to her.

But regardless of how powerful or weird it had been, it was meaningless, he told himself. She might be one of the most beautiful women he'd ever laid eyes on, but she wasn't the kind of woman he meshed with and that had been brought home to him as they'd talked at the reception.

The kind of woman he meshed with was full of life, free-spirited, lively and adventurous, outgoing and game for anything—like him. The kind of woman he meshed with would have flirted audaciously with him when Marti had introduced them. She would never have taken seriously his joking about her occupation, and probably would have shot back a few innuendos of her own.

But a prim reverend's granddaughter? A woman who held herself so stiff and straight she could have had a pole running up the zipper of her bridesmaid's dress? A woman who not only hadn't found the fact that he'd been hurt on a skateboard funny, but who had given him the impression that she thought it was just a stupid, childish thing to have done? A woman who was that reserved and subdued and stuffy?

Huh-uh. No thanks.

He'd tried it with a few women like that, and he knew they were not for him. That his personality, the way he liked to live his life, clashed with theirs and their expectations of who he should be and how he should behave.

So even if Kate Perry was a beauty, even if he *had* gotten a kick out of the verbal back-and-forth with her and the evidence that she was clearly nobody's fool, he wasn't interested.

Besides, there was also the fact that she lived in Northbridge and that she was Marti's sister-in-law.

Northbridge was not a place he wanted to be tethered to any more than he had to be to take care of his grandmother.

And messing with an in-law's sibling? He'd already been dumb enough to hook up with someone with that kind of family connection—Wyatt's first wife's sister. And when it didn't work out? Backlash and awkwardness to spare. Not to mention strain on his relationship with Wyatt.

So as far as he was concerned, Kate Perry was a no-go all the way around.

Well, except that she was doing his massage tonight.

If he didn't have to have his shoulder loosened up so it didn't hurt like hell, he would cancel that appointment—there was no question about it.

But he really needed the massage, no matter who was

giving it; otherwise, he was going to have to pop pain pills and he didn't want to do that.

Still, he was a little worried about what might happen—purely involuntarily—when someone who looked like Kate Perry touched him.

But he just had to suck it up and have the massage.

Maybe if he kept reminding himself over and over again just how not-for-him Kate Perry was, it would help.

But just in case it didn't, he was keeping his pants on and letting her deal with the shoulder and nothing but the shoulder.

Get in there, get it done, get out.

That was what Kate told herself as she stood outside the door to the treatment room in the office she shared with the local chiropractor.

The receptionist had just taken Ry Grayson to the treatment room, given him his instructions and left for the day. The chiropractor wasn't in on Mondays. That meant that there were now only two people in the office—Kate and Ry Grayson, who was waiting for his massage.

A massage that would be no different than any massage she'd ever given because he was just a client, she told herself.

So why was she dreading it so much?

Or was she feeling something else?

No, it was dread. It had to be dread. Why would it be anything else? Anything like excitement to see him again?

It wouldn't be.

And even if it was, she wasn't having any part of it.

She was husband-hunting. She wanted what she'd always wanted—to find the one man she could build her life with. The one man who would want what she wanted—to get married, to buy a house, to settle down and have a family, to raise that family together. And she was tired of being distracted from that goal by men who ultimately—even if they said it was what they wanted—didn't want that same thing.

Steady, stable, serious, rock solid—that was the kind of man she was looking for. Someone who was clear in his convictions, who knew himself and what he wanted. Someone like her.

Certainly, someone who wouldn't mislead her into thinking he *did* want what she wanted and then just string her along.

And any man who gave her the slightest indication that that wasn't who he was, absolutely was not a contender. Absolutely was not someone she was putting an ounce of energy or a minute of her time into. Because doing that three—*three*—times was enough. More than enough—three engagements that ended short of the altar were more than any one person's limit.

So no more fly-by-nights.

Or, as in the case of Ry Grayson and his arrival for yesterday's wedding, no more fly-by-days, either.

His own sister had said that he was just a kid at heart, that she didn't think he would ever grow up. And even if Kate hadn't had a preconceived belief that that was the kind of man he was, Marti saying it was a glaring warning that Kate was not taking lightly. In fact, she didn't need any more confirmation than that to cement Ry Grayson on the do-not-touch-with-a-ten-foot-pole list.

So, all right, maybe he *had* gotten to her a little at the wedding and maybe that was why what she was feeling could possibly be excitement at the prospect of seeing him again. Opening up to her, letting her know he liked her brother, confiding his feelings about his sister's late fiancé—there was no denying that the man could be charming and appealing.

But she'd learned—*three times*—that charm and appeal didn't get her to the altar. And she couldn't let charm or appeal blind her again. She had a goal, she was unwavering in her pursuit of that goal and that was all there was to it. She absolutely would not allow herself to be waylaid by anyone she honestly didn't believe was a potential life partner.

And when it came to this massage, she was a professional and she could do this and keep it purely in that arena—business as usual. And no business-as-usual massage excited her.

With that sorted through in her mind, Kate set her shoulders straight and imagined her goals and resolve protecting her like a shield from Ry Grayson's charm and appeal. She took several deep breaths for strength and to clear her mind. And then she knocked firmly on the door.

"I'm indecent, come on in."

Well, no one had ever said *that* before.

Kate suppressed a smile and went in.

"Hi. Sorry if I kept you waiting," she said unapologetically.

"I think I dozed off, so even if you did keep me waiting, I didn't know it."

He was lying facedown on the massage table, his arms at his sides. He hadn't used the sheet he'd been given to cover up with, probably because he was still wearing everything from the waist down. But he was naked from the waist up. Naked, tanned, muscular and broad-shouldered at the top of an impressive V that narrowed to his waist and an equally impressive rear end that she almost wished he hadn't left encased in jeans because one look at his backside and a slight shiver ran up her arms.

"Is it cold in here?" she asked.

"I'm fine," he said.

"As long as you're comfortable," she lied to cover her own reaction.

Business as usual, she reminded herself.

"Which shoulder is giving you trouble?" she asked, moving closer to the side of the table.

"The left," he answered.

"I can use oil or lotion—which would you prefer?"

"Makes no difference to me."

Kate chose oil, pouring some into her hands to warm it and trying as she did not to admire the pure, raw masculine magnificence of those shoulders and that back that could make a person drool, and biceps that were honed and carved and looked as if they were amply able to pull his body weight and more up the sheer sides of mountains.

Business as usual.

She went from the side of the table to the head of it.

"Fancy feet!" he exclaimed the minute she was in position and he could see her from the opening of the headrest. "Polish and a toe ring? That's a surprise."

Leave it to him to say something about it.

"The polish was for the wedding—open-toed shoes. And the ring has been there for so long it won't come off," she said as if there was no more to it.

But the truth was, she'd refreshed the polish, and she never tried to take off the ring. She just didn't want him to know that she secretly liked that thin, silver bit of nonconformity that had come out of her late teens.

She also didn't mention the fact that his view would

have ordinarily consisted of only clunky clogs, but that she'd opted for sandals today. With him in mind, although she didn't want to admit it even to herself.

"I'm going to touch you now," she warned because sometimes her clients liked to know in advance.

"Go for it," he said with a laugh that managed to sound sexy even through the slight muffle of the headrest.

"I'm pretty strong, so if I hurt you at all, let me know right away."

"Give me all you've got, I think I can take it."

And yet her hands hovered over his shoulders.

You said you were going to touch him, now do it!

It was just that she had some concerns about what touching him was going to do to her. Maybe nothing—after all, she'd never had any kind of personal reaction to touching anyone else. But Ry Grayson? There was something different about him.

Still, she had no choice, so she took a deep breath and laid her hands on his shoulders.

Another wave of those shivers went from her palms all the way up her arms again. But she put every effort into ignoring it. And when she did, she began to get an idea of what she was dealing with therapeutically.

"Wow, those are some big, hard knots," she said.

"Big and hard—isn't that supposed to be a good thing?" he countered with another laugh.

The man was definitely incorrigible.

Kate took her hands away. "I'm going to have to loosen the knots with some heat before I can deal with them," she informed him without acknowledging his remark.

Then she escaped from the room and collapsed silently against the wall just outside the door.

She took more deep breaths. She told herself she was being ridiculous. She told herself again why she could not allow herself to be affected like this by Ry Grayson.

But only after about the sixth deep breath did she feel strong enough to cross the hall to the supply area of the office and continue with what she was supposed to be doing.

She took some hot packs from a drawer and heated them in the microwave. Then she retrieved two warm, damp towels from the Crock-Pot where she kept them heating, and went back to the treatment room.

On went the first towel, then the heat packs, then the second towel over them.

And the moan that came from Ry Grayson in response sounded much too much like the kind of moan he might make during the course of far more intimate activities.

Kate swallowed with some difficulty, pressed herself flat against the wall inside the room this time and decided to try polite, innocuous conversation to keep her mind and her reactions to him on another path.

"Did your grandmother end up making it through everything yesterday without any upset?" she asked.

"She did okay, actually. She's pretty fond of Noah and she was glad to see Marti happy again."

"And she was all right with Marti leaving on her honeymoon? I know Marti was worried about how Theresa would handle it."

"There's a reason for that—Gram is up and down, and we never know how she'll handle anything. But Marti and Wyatt both leaving this morning didn't seem to bother her. She was almost chipper all the way through lunch today. Then she took a nap and had a nightmare she keeps having—I don't know how much Noah has told you about what's going on with Gram."

"He didn't think it was a secret—especially since we are all family now." Kate threw in that reminder again for her own sake and for his. "I know that when your grandmother was seventeen her parents died and she ended up being taken in by Hector Tyson and his wife. That he bought a major chunk of land from her for a song and got rich himself from selling it off in lots, and then also selling all the building materials for the houses that were built on it because he's always been the only game in town when it came to lumber and hardware—"

"Something we're going to change by opening a Home-Max—which he doesn't like."

"I know that when Theresa first came to Northbridge, she said it was to get back something that was taken from her," Kate continued. "And that your family thought she was talking about the land. But when Marti and Noah told Theresa that Marti is pregnant, your grandmother got really upset and claimed that Hector seduced her and that she had his baby—"

"And we believe her, especially since Marti talked to some woman named Emmalina—"

"She was the wife of the minister at the time," Kate filled him in.

"Right. And this Emmalina said Gram went to talk to the minister, that while she waited for him, she talked to Emmalina about being in love with a married man. And between the things she said and the fact that Gram was all wrapped up in a big coat on a warm day, we believe she was hiding a pregnancy," Ry said.

"Noah also told me that Theresa says Hector took her

baby from her before she even saw it or held it or knew if it was a boy or a girl."

"We still aren't sure if that's a figment of Gram's imagination or not."

"But if it's true, then that baby—which would be as old as our parents by now—could be what Theresa wants back," Kate concluded.

"So you know plenty."

"Am I not supposed to?" Kate asked, hoping she hadn't gotten her brother into trouble.

"No, it's fine. Anyway, this dream Gram has is that the baby is crying for her. She has problems with depression most of the time but when she has this dream, she really gets bummed out. She ended up crying all afternoon and there was nothing her nurse Mary Pat or I could do to cheer her up."

"I feel so badly for her," Kate said. She couldn't imagine how awful it would be to have a child and then have it taken from her.

"Yeah, it's lousy," Ry agreed.

It was definitely easier to talk to him without looking at that handsome face, with his back draped in towels, without touching him while the heat packs did their job, and Kate was feeling more herself.

"We've notified this Tyson character that we intend to sue him for restitution over the land," Ry went on to say. "Our lawyers are putting the finishing touches on that this week, but I think I'm going to have to take the bull by the horns over the baby. Do you know Tyson?"

Kate decided enough time had passed with the heat packs applied to his shoulders and since she felt she could better deal with massaging him, she removed the towels and packs. But before she answered Ry's question, she warmed more oil between her hands and said, "I'm going to start on your spine to get everything in line before I work on your shoulder."

"Sure, whatever," he said.

Talking to him about his grandmother *had* helped dispel some of her reaction to him because this time when she began the massage, she had something to think about other than how smooth and sleek his skin was.

"Yes, I know Hector Tyson," she said then, finally responding to what he'd asked. "Everyone does. He's a cranky old man like my grandfather. In fact, I'll be seeing Hector as soon as we're done here. I'm sure you know about that holding barn he bought out from under you to try to keep Home-Max from coming in?"

"Yeah, I know about that."

"Well, he's closed on the deal and he wants the title. I agreed to deliver it to him tonight."

"You're a masseuse who moonlights as a messenger?"

"I'm a masseuse who's also the city clerk."

"Seriously?"

"The city clerk job in Northbridge is only a part-time position—we just aren't big enough to need one full-time. And since being a masseuse in a small town is also not a huge moneymaker, I do both jobs."

"Ah, that's why you were only here this afternoon, not this morning," he said, although his *ah* was tinged with some pleasure as she worked her way from his waist upward and began to address those wide shoulders of his, paying particular attention to the injured one.

"So why don't I go with you when we're finished here and you can introduce me?" he suggested then.

"I can think of about 100 reasons why not," she answered before thinking better of it.

"Why is that?"

Of course he would ask, and now that her runaway mouth had gotten her into it, what was she going to say? That she was worried about her own visceral responses to him? That she didn't want to risk what might happen if she was with him any more than necessary? That the rock-solid muscles of his back were not the kind of "rock solid" she was looking for and so she considered him a waste of her valuable time?

"I just don't think that would be a good idea," she hedged. "I'm going to Hector's house as a civil servant. I can't bring a *date*."

"Who said anything about a date?"

She wished she hadn't.

"No one," she backpedaled. "I'm just saying that that's what it would look like to Hector. And then you'd attack him and—"

"I'm not going to *attack* an old man. I just want to talk to him. Wouldn't it be better to start off with an introduction from someone he knows? Someone who can say I'm *family* now?"

She didn't appreciate having *that* table turned on her. But she did know that her brother would want her to help the Graysons in any way she could, especially in getting to the bottom of things for Theresa.

Plus now that she'd shot off her mouth about going to Hector Tyson's house tonight and then made the other slips of the tongue that had compounded things, if she didn't concede, this was apt to become a much bigger deal than she wanted it to. And then that could get back to her brother and it all just seemed like it could snowball if she didn't bite the bullet and let Ry Grayson have his way....

"Ouch!"

"Oh, I'm sorry," she said, not realizing that in the process of working on his shoulder her own frustration might have made her rougher than she should have been.

She was more careful as she stretched his arm toward his back.

"So what do you say?" he asked. "Will you do the honors with old man Tyson? Otherwise I'm just gonna follow you from here so I know how to get to his place and we'll end up there at the same time anyway."

"You weren't planning to go tonight until you heard I was going," she accused.

"But now that I know you are, I might as well trail you—it's easier than finding him on my own. So what'll it be? Together with an introduction—the way a *family* member would do with another family member? Or some awkward, coincidental, synchronized arrival on the old man's doorstep that'll be harder for you to explain?"

Kate was finished with his massage and rather than be quick about answering him, she left the room to get another warm, damp towel. As she laid it across his back and shoulders when she returned, she sighed elaborately and said, "I suppose—since you *are* family now—you can tag along."

"Not gracious, but I'll take it," he said.

After another few minutes of silence that she let lapse to make it clear she didn't appreciate being coerced into something she didn't want to do, Kate used the damp towel while it was still warm to rub the oil off his back, hating that it gave her a tiny thrill to do it and to hear his sighs of satisfaction when she did.

And now her time with him wasn't going to end here, she thought, knowing that it was also not a good sign that that excitement she'd been trying to dress up as dread in anticipation of his massage had returned with the prospect of taking him with her to Hector Tyson's house.

But the massage and taking him to Hector's house were one-time and one-time-only occurrences, she told herself. After this, there wouldn't be any reason for her to even see Ry Grayson, let alone spend time with him. Or touch him.

If she could just get through the next hour or so, this would all be over with and she could go back to her single-minded husband-hunting.

That meant going home to her apartment to check the two Internet dating services she'd joined, and looking through the catalog of men she'd received in the mail today from Partner-Finders—the matchmaking firm she'd signed up with in Billings.

Stubborn determination—that's what she had. Stubborn determination to find herself a mate.

And she wasn't going to let Ry Grayson get in the way of it.

Even if the feel of every taut tendon and hard muscle of his back seemed burned indelibly into her brain.

Chapter Three

"I told you people before and I'll tell you again," Hector Tyson shouted, "these are nothing but the ramblings of a crazy woman and no, there was no baby, let alone one that I took away from her! And I don't need to talk to anybody who's threatening to sue me and trying to put me out of business on top of it!"

The old man redirected his venom from Ry to Kate. "First your brother Noah brought that Grayson woman he just married and now you bring this Grayson. If you Perrys don't quit bringing them to my house, you're not going to be welcome here, either! Now both of you get out!"

"I'm sorry we upset you, Hector," Kate said, "but—"

"But nothing! Just get out!"

Kate wasn't fond of Hector Tyson but she also didn't like having been a part of aggravating him. And since the man was eighty-four years old and his face was now the color of beet juice with a vein throbbing in his temple, she was worried he might have a stroke or a heart attack.

"Let's go," she urged Ry, who was glaring at the cantankerous old man.

"I'll leave," he told Hector, "but don't think this is over by any means. I believe there *was* a baby and I'm going to find out what happened to it, if it's the last thing I ever do."

"That's not making it better," Kate pointed out. "Let's just go."

Ry apparently felt the need to give Hector the hard stare for another moment. The hard stare that Hector was returning unwaveringly from squinted eyes.

But after that additional moment, Ry turned on his heels and went with Kate from the living room, across the entrance hall and through the front door of the Tyson home.

"Well, that was pleasant," she said facetiously once they were outside in the fresh evening air again.

Ry laughed. "Ah, come on, you can't tell me anything to do with that guy is ever pleasant. You said yourself that he's cranky."

Kate was surprised by how quickly Ry could switch gears. He'd been arguing heatedly with Hector for the last twenty minutes, but now he was once again as calm and relaxed as he'd been before meeting the surly elderly man.

"Was that all an act in there?" she asked as they walked to her car. Ry had ridden his motorcycle to his massage so Kate had driven them to Hector Tyson's house.

"An act?" he parroted.

"I thought you were as mad as Hector was and now you're happy as a clam again."

"Ooh, clams sound good," he said as he opened the

driver's side door for her and waited for her to get in. "I'd like to wring that old coot's scrawny neck, but I'm not mad at you, so why would I take it out on you? Or let it ruin the rest of this warm summer night?"

That was reasonable. And levelheaded. "I'm glad you didn't take it out on me. I'm just surprised that you can shake it off so easily."

He shrugged. "I didn't expect this to be amiable. It went about the way I thought it would. No sense stewing or brooding over it."

Or throwing a tantrum, which was what she'd come to expect from men in her past and had thought she might be in line for again now. But Ry merely closed her door and went around the front end of her small sedan.

As he did, her eyes went with him, drinking in the view of him in jeans and a plain white crew-neck T-shirt that fitted him like a second skin and seemed to throw into relief not only that back she'd had her hands on such a short while ago, but also a chest and a set of flat, to-die-for washboard abs. And he didn't brood, stew or throw tantrums. Kate appreciated that.

He got into the passenger seat then and once again said, "Clams—let's have some. I don't suppose there's a seafood restaurant around here."

"Sorry," she said, wondering if he was just assuming they were going to go to dinner now.

"How about pizza, then?" he suggested enthusiastically. "Sometimes I can get clams on pizza and if I can't have 'em fresh, that'll do."

"There *is* a pizza place, but I've never noticed if clams are one of the toppings they offer."

"Let me guess—because you only eat cheese pizza."

"I eat more on my pizza than just cheese, but I've never eaten clams at all, let alone that way."

"Then you don't know what you're missing. What do you say—shall we go see if we can get a pizza with clams? You can broaden your horizons."

"Dinner wasn't part of this errand tonight," she pointed out. "And what makes you think that I don't have other plans?"

"Do you?"

"I have things to do at home." There was that catalog of men waiting for her.

"One of the things you have to do at home is eat, though, right?"

"Yes."

"So eat with me and then go home and do your *things.* I'll buy you dinner as payment for taking me to meet Tyson."

Besides the sandals on her fancy feet, she was dressed in navy blue scrubs—the clothes she worked in because the hospital preferred that anyone providing any kind of health services wear them. And while she *had* paid special attention to her makeup today and wound her hair into a loose knot at her crown that left wisps of curls around her face, it was the scrubs she was thinking of when she said, "I'm not dressed to go out to eat."

"Come on, you can't tell me that there's a dress code to eat pizza in Northbridge," he cajoled as Kate started the engine and backed out of Hector Tyson's driveway.

She knew she shouldn't agree to have dinner with him. But there *were* only leftovers for her at home. And she *did* love pizza....

"It's just having a friendly meal together—surely we can do that?" he said as if he knew she was considering it.

"Friendly?" she repeated.

"Nothing but," he swore zealously.

Friendly was safe. His zeal was a little disappointing somehow, but she didn't want to analyze why that should be and instead merely told herself that as long as things between them could be friendly and nothing more, she could have dinner with him. Friendly was not going to gum up anything for her.

"I suppose I could do pizza. If it doesn't take too long. And you *do* owe me for getting me into trouble with Hector."

"Yeah, I know how you Good Girls avoid trouble," he said. "I probably owe you a salad and a soda, too. And maybe my left kidney and my firstborn child."

"Just the pizza will be enough," she said wryly.

They were back on Main Street by then. She drove past the redbrick corner building that housed the small medical facility where she worked and where his motorcycle was parked, and went to the pizza parlor instead, coming to a stop nose-first at the curb there.

"Is this still open?" Ry asked since they could see through the storefront windows that the place was empty.

"Sure. But it's after eight—most people in Northbridge have finished dinner and it's too early yet for late-night snacking."

"But not by much, I'll bet," Ry muttered as he got out of her car.

Once inside they chose a table in the center of the small establishment and within moments, Ry had discovered clams on the long list of available toppings.

"I suppose they'll come out of a can, and fresh are a whole other experience, but let's have them anyway," he decreed. "Or shall I just get them on half so you can have something else?"

"I think anything that has you in this much rapture had better be tried," Kate said indulgently.

"Rapture?" he repeated with a crooked smile. "You think this is rapture? This is nothing but a little yen for clams."

Kate wasn't about to explore what he considered rapture to be, so instead—when their pizza was ordered and their drinks were served—she said, "If you *do* believe there was a baby between your grandmother and Hector, and you want to find it, what's your plan?"

He obviously had one because he didn't need to think about it before he said, "I know adoption records—especially from that far back—are sealed, but I've been thinking that maybe I'll use the computer to access what I can of newspaper articles and birth announcements at the time. See if anything seems like a clue to who could have acquired a baby that didn't seem to be their birth child. I could also comb over old records and compare births to census reports from around here—maybe that will tell me whose family grew even though there's no record of the mother having given birth."

"I don't mean to be a naysayer, but that sounds like trying to find a needle in a haystack. And the fact that it was over fifty years ago won't help anything."

"You know what *would* help things, though?"

"Hmm?" Kate asked as she sipped her iced tea.

"If I knew the city clerk—that *is* who oversees and has access to anything that's a matter of public record, like census reports and births—isn't it?"

"Did you have this up your sleeve all along?" she accused.

"I found out you were the city clerk when I was shirtless—just a couple of hours ago. So no sleeves have been involved in this," he deadpanned.

"You didn't know I was the city clerk before that?" Kate persisted.

"Sorry to disappoint you when I'm sure you'd be happier if you could believe I was calculating and conniving, but this really was coincidental."

"Why would I be happier if I could believe you were calculating and conniving?"

He shrugged. "It's just the sense I get from you—that you want not to like me."

Great, he was intuitive, too.

But why did the idea that she was trying not to like him seem to strike him as amusing?

"You're smiling," she observed. "You have the sense that I want not to like you and you find that funny?"

"And challenging—which is dangerous for me because I can never resist a challenge."

That comment went unexplored when their pizza arrived just then and Ry was intent on her tasting it and telling him what she thought.

"I love it!" she said without disguising her own shock at finding it true. Since she wasn't a big fan of seafood, she'd expected to dislike clams on pizza.

Ry grinned but looked as stunned as she was by her declaration. "Really?"

"The tomato and the clams together have this sort of buttery richness—honestly, I love it."

"If you think this is good, someday you'll have to have linguine and clam sauce made with fresh clams—*that's* something."

After a few more bites, rather than returning to the subject of her not wanting to like him, he said, "So, how about it? Can I look through your records?"

He made that sound seductive, which caused Kate to roll her eyes as if he were beyond redemption, and turn a bit preachy. "They aren't *my* records. They're city records. And since they're public, they're available to anyone who wants to look through them."

"Tomorrow?"

"I'll be at that office tomorrow afternoon. The records department is in the courthouse building on the corner of Main Street and South—"

"I know where it is. But how late are you open? I'm swamped with Home-Max stuff tomorrow so it's going to be tough for me to get away, but I want to jump on this."

"Government offices close at five."

He laughed. "Geez, loosen up, will you? You sound like a recorded phone message."

Had she stiffened at the prospect of seeing him again tomorrow?

Probably. It was just that he made it so easy to be with him and she knew that was a pitfall.

She put some effort into outwardly relaxing, though, and announced that she was breaking her one-slice-of-pizza rule and having half of a second slice.

"Go for it!" he encouraged, taking a full second slice of his own.

Then, as if he were slightly baffled, he said, "So, city clerk, I can see that job for you. But how did you decide to become a masseuse?"

"A therapeutic massage therapist," she corrected because once more he'd made *masseuse* sound a little off-color. "I wanted to do something in health care but I didn't want to be a doctor or a nurse—I wanted something that wouldn't take too much dedication so that when I have a family, my family can genuinely come first. Being a physical therapist or a chiropractor seemed to offer more flexibility, but Northbridge already has one of each of those, and the town isn't big enough to support more than that. But there was no massage therapist."

"You wanted a career in health care but you actually chose what line based on what Northbridge needed, not on what you wanted? As if Northbridge is the only place you could get a job?"

"It's the only place I intend to live, so, yes," she said matter-of-factly.

"There's a great big world out there, you know?"

"But I want to live here."

"And the whole flexible-hours issue so you could devote yourself to a family you don't even have yet? You let a lot of outside things dictate your choice."

"I just thought it through and made my decision based on what I want for myself now and in the future. You find that odd?"

He shrugged. "That just isn't the way I do things. I like to make choices based on the moment, on going with the flow of things as they happen, on what feels right."

"Is this the first time it's occurred to you that we're different?"

He laughed, pushing his plate away after his third slice of pizza and lounging slightly in his chair while Kate continued to sit very straight in hers.

"Believe me, I know we're very different," he said then, his tone wry.

"You say that as if I have a tail or green scales for skin," she pointed out.

"No green scales—your skin is like cream. And your tail

is one of the finest I've ever seen. But damn, you're serious. What if things don't work out the way you think they will? What if you don't ever get married and have a family? What if a tornado strikes and there's no more Northbridge? Will you be able to be happy doing massages anyway or will you regret that you didn't do something you actually wanted to do?"

"I know that some of life just happens to you, no matter what you do. But I also believe that if you set your priorities and go after what you want with steadfast, single-minded determination, you can achieve your goals. I'm just making accommodations for those goals in advance so that when I achieve them, there won't be obstacles already mucking them up."

He studied her for a long moment, smiling a Cheshire cat smile right before he said, "You're just so centered and sure of yourself and what you want and where you're going, aren't you? You think you have everything under control."

"As much as possible," she confirmed.

He shook his head and grinned. "God help me, there's a part of me that wants to rattle that cage you're in. Who put you there—the Reverend or your parents or a bad experience with a man?"

The waitress appeared just then to ask if they wanted to take the remainder of the pizza. Ry didn't but Kate did, and while the waitress boxed it for her, Ry glanced at the bill and handed the money to the waitress when she was done.

"I am not in a cage," Kate felt compelled to say once the waitress had left them alone again.

"Boxed, caged, tied up—any way you want to look at, you're contained."

Kate merely shook her head. "From your perspective.

From mine, I'm doing just fine, thank you very much. And I certainly don't need my *cage rattled*. Especially not by you," she warned.

He smiled again and Kate had the feeling that every word she said only made her more of a challenge.

"Right, I get it," he said. "I'm not your type. Don't worry, you aren't mine, either."

That stung. Kate had no idea why, but it did.

She felt her spine stiffen in response. "Well, now that we have *that* settled, we should probably go."

He grinned as if he knew that her back was up. "Yeah, since there are so many people lined up waiting for this table," he said with a glance around them at the still empty restaurant.

He stood, though, and so did Kate, making sure to take the pizza box with her. But before Ry moved away from the table, he rolled his injured shoulder and seeing it sent a flash of memory through her mind of his naked back.

"You *are* good at what you do, I'll give you that," he said. "I feel a lot better."

"So maybe my occupation wasn't such a bad choice."

"I didn't say it was a *bad* choice," he countered, leaving tip money on the table. "If I were you, I'd just be a little worried about what went into making it and if it was the *right* choice."

"It was for me," Kate said decisively.

Ry motioned for her to go ahead of him to the door and as she did he said from behind, "So, do you ever do massages that aren't for medicinal reasons—like they do at spas?" he asked, apparently to make it clear it was not a goad, but a genuine question.

So that was the way Kate took it. "Sure. I have some clients who just want the pampering aspect. And one Saturday a month I run spa day—I put candles around the office, offer teas and treats. The local manicurist comes in to do pedicures, one of our hairstylists is there for scalp treatments and deep conditioning, and we do as much of a spa kind of atmosphere as I can work out in a medical office."

"Girls only?"

"It isn't a rule, but we've never had a man come. And if we did, it probably *would* make everyone padding around in bathrobes, with towels on their heads and toe separators on their feet, a little uncomfortable."

They were at the front end of her car by then and Ry stopped, nodding up the street in the direction of the hospital. "I'll walk back for my wheels so you can get right home to those *things* I kept you from."

Why did the idea of getting on Internet dating sites and looking through a catalog of potential mates suddenly seem anticlimactic to the way she'd just spent the last few hours?

Kate tried to ignore it.

"Thanks for the massage," Ry said then. "And for taking me to meet Tyson. Sorry about him slapping your wrists for bringing me."

"The pizza made up for it—thanks for that. And for introducing me to clams."

He grinned. "Sure. I'll have to think of what else I can slide between the bars of your cage to open your eyes to things outside of it."

Kate again shook her head and once more rolled her eyes. But, for some reason, she also smiled a little.

"I'll see you tomorrow," she said, knowing that shouldn't

be something that somehow brightened her outlook on the coming day, but realizing that it did.

"Will you wait for me if I'm a little late?" he asked in a tone that held an enticement all its own.

"We're talking government office, remember? It closes at five sharp."

"Come on—small town, you're the city clerk, I'm betting you have the key to the office door and can make your own hours."

"I *could* but why would I?"

"Just to help out? I have a full 18-wheeler coming in from Missoula tomorrow that has to be completely unloaded so it can get back tomorrow night. I'll be lucky to get to you by five but then there's that needle in a haystack to look for. How about if I bring dinner and we eat it while we both go through the old records?"

"Oh, now not only am I extending my office hours to suit you, I'm helping you look through the records, too?"

"Think of my poor, suffering grandmother," he said like a line in a bad melodrama.

What she was thinking about was how good he looked in the glow of the streetlight he was standing under. How sharply cut were the lines of his face.

Which was precisely why she should say no.

But before she'd said anything at all, he repeated, "Think of my poor, suffering grandmother. Think of the clams," he added equally as melodramatically.

And she laughed in spite of herself and heard herself say, "For Theresa and the clams, I suppose."

He grinned again, drawing her attention to his mouth and making her suddenly wonder what it might be like to have him kiss her. She had no doubt that he would have a flair when it came to that the way he did with every-thing else.

But those thoughts were uncalled for and not at all what she wanted to be thinking about!

"Just try to get there as early as possible, I have *things* to do at home tomorrow night, too," she said sternly to counteract her own mental wanderings.

"The minute I can get away, I'll be there," he assured.

Friendly—that was all tonight was supposed to be and all it had ended up being, Kate lectured herself. It was all tomorrow night would be. They'd agreed they weren't each other's types and she was beginning to believe it because while there was a flirtatious undertone to almost everything he said, he didn't go anywhere with it. It didn't seem to be leading to anything like that kissing she couldn't seem to get her mind off of.

She was still trying like mad, though, as she said, "I'll see you when you get there, then."

"No, I'll see *you* when I get there," he countered as if it were a game.

Because everything *was* more of a game to him than it was to her, she reminded herself.

Reinforcing that notion, he winked at her. Devilishly. Charmingly. Mischievously. Then he slipped his hands into his jean pockets, turned and began to amble in the di-rection of the hospital.

And Kate was suddenly left looking at that great rear end of his for the second time today.

Set into motion, it was an even better view and all at once the memory of his massage flooded her brain in a way no other massage had ever come back to her.

Vividly. As if her hands were on him again at that very

moment. She recalled how his skin had felt, how hard every bulging muscle had been, how taut and tight and sleek each and every inch of his back was.

Stop it! she silently commanded, forcing her gaze off him, making herself move to her car door.

But once she was behind the wheel and heading up Main Street again, there he was, just reaching his motorcycle to swing a long leg over the seat before he caught sight of her and waved.

And even as she waved in return, she was thinking that he'd been right about one thing tonight and wrong about another.

He'd been right when he'd assumed she wanted not to like him.

But that part about him not being her type?

That wasn't really true.

The truth was, he was *exactly* her type.

But it was a type she would swear on a stack of bibles that she was not going to fall for again.

Chapter Four

"I think we're just going to have to admit it—after all this, we're not finding the needle in the haystack," Ry decreed.

Kate was relieved that he was finally admitting it. They'd been going through records since just before five o'clock on Tuesday afternoon and it was after nine when he conceded that they hadn't found a baby unaccounted for during the time period Theresa claimed she'd given birth, a baby Hector Tyson might have taken from her.

"I'm sorry," Kate said simply. But they'd gone through everything on the computer, and even through aged paper documents that had yet to be converted to computer records, without coming up with anything suspicious.

"And I told you I did stuff on the Internet most of last night," Ry said. "I combed over old newspaper items until nearly dawn but this whole effort has been a bust."

"Yes, you did tell me," Kate confirmed sympathetically.

"Just how bad a guy is this Tyson character?" Ry asked then, pushing out of the desk chair he'd been occupying.

Once he was on his feet he arched his spine, flexed his shoulders backward and did a stretch that Kate tried not to watch too intently. Still, she was grateful when he was finished and began to pace.

"Is it possible," he went on, "that Tyson could have... done harm to the baby rather than giving it away?"

"Oh, I can't imagine that," Kate said in revulsion at the thought. "Hector is a lot of things, but a baby-killer? I just don't think so."

She was hesitant to say what *was* going through her mind, though, and so she just watched Ry take long strides back and forth on his sturdy legs.

He wasn't dressed in anything special—jeans and a gray polo shirt—and she knew he'd probably been in those clothes since early that morning when he'd met the Home-Max truck. Yet he still looked great, even with his sculpted face slightly shadowed with beard. She didn't always like the look of stubble but on Ry it was so sexy it was almost unbearable.

"I don't know," he said in relation to nothing more than his own agitation and frustration as far as she could tell.

"Is it possible," Kate ventured, "that Hector isn't lying when he says there was no baby?"

"Sure, it's possible," he said.

Kate had worried that he might bite off her head at the suggestion but he hadn't and she was glad to learn that wasn't something she had to expect from him.

"Gram is delusional," he continued. "There's no denying that. There have been times when she thinks something from a TV show has happened to her. But the delusions don't last. In fact, they're pretty easily shot down. But this is different. It's just so much bigger—sneaking out of her house in Missoula, stealing Mary Pat's car to drive here by herself when she's usually afraid to even go onto the porch alone? Hiding out in the old, decaying house where she grew up? Staring for hours through the windows, thinking she might see some sign of her lost child? And there are the dreams and her insistence that she get back what was taken from her, the shame she feels, the way we've had to coax her to tell us anything at all? None of it is her usual behavior. My every sense, whenever I can get her anywhere near the subject, is that it's real and I won't give up on her until I'm convinced that it isn't."

Kate couldn't help appreciating the fact that something that was so important to Theresa was being taken this seriously when it might easily have been disregarded as just another manifestation of the elderly woman's mental illness.

"I suppose Tyson could have taken the baby out of Northbridge altogether," Ry postulated. "From what Gram told Marti when she finally talked about there being a baby, it sounded like it was delivered at home—at Tyson's house, we're assuming. But there's nothing that says the baby stayed in Northbridge."

"No, I don't suppose there is. But that would make it so much more difficult to find."

"It would have been harder for Tyson, too, though. Northbridge has to have been his comfort zone. Keeping the baby here, maybe placing it with people he had a hold over—that would have given him the best chance of controlling things, wouldn't it?"

"I would think so," Kate agreed.

"And there's no sense looking beyond Northbridge

until I'm sure I've exhausted every avenue *in* North-bridge. So what about something under-the-table *in* Northbridge?"

"Something under-the-table?" Kate repeated.

"Would you put it past Tyson to forge a birth certificate or pull some kind of strings or call in a favor to make it look like the baby he gave someone was really their own? To have the adoptive parents' names put on the birth certificate so that now, just going through records, that's all we find—things that seem to be on the up-and-up?"

"*That* I wouldn't put past Hector, no," Kate said. "You already know that he wasn't above doing whatever it was he did—whether it was lying to your grandmother or blackmailing her or just using her grief over her parents' deaths—to get her to sell all that land to him for next to nothing. Hector has a reputation for doing anything to get what he wants, to get his own way. He pressures and coerces and threatens City Council members, he's never been above bullying anyone. Certainly, if someone owes him something, he doesn't forget it and he expects to be paid in any way he sees fit. And he's always been a man with influence—even through hard times, he's had more money than anyone and that's brought him power."

"Plus, adoptions weren't handled as openly all those years ago as they are now," Ry said, picking up where Kate had left off. "A lot of times adopted kids weren't even told they were adopted. Tyson might not have had to force the parents to keep quiet, to accept a doctored birth certificate. The parents might have been just as glad not to have it known that the baby wasn't their own."

"I could see that, yes," Kate conceded.

"Or there might have even been some story to explain

the sudden appearance of a baby—like that a relative had had it and couldn't raise it or hadn't wanted it."

"Again, sure."

"And *because* Northbridge is a small town, there would have been talk—whispers, if a couple suddenly became proud parents without there being a pregnancy beforehand to account for it, or open gossip if anyone inherited a baby for some reason, right?"

"Right."

"Only after a while, that talk would die down," he continued forming this theory out loud. "And after it died down, it would be forgotten about, the baby would just be a part of whatever family it had come into. Then, over the years—especially fifty-plus of them—the fact that that child had made a sudden, even a mysterious appearance, would be mostly forgotten about."

"I imagine so," Kate concurred.

"But someone who was around then might remember it with some prompting. So what we need to do is to find that someone."

We....

The entire day, whenever Kate had realized she was looking forward to seeing him again tonight, she'd taken herself to task about it. She'd reminded herself that she was not to waste time with Ry Grayson. That she had something important to put her energies into and that he was not it. She'd assured herself that this foray into the records would be the last she saw of him. And while her immediate inclination now that she was face-to-face with the energetic, charismatic man was to let herself be caught up in his enthusiasm, she couldn't do that.

So she said, "Hold on. Yesterday's massage was my

job. Sifting through the records today—also my job. I've accommodated you in both instances by extending my hours, but this is it for me. You're on your own from here."

That stopped his pacing cold. He glanced at her, frowning as endearingly as an ornery puppy. "Aw, really? You're gonna bail on me just when we're becoming a team? When we're getting so good at brainstorming together?"

She didn't know how true that was, but it pleased her much too much to hear him say it.

Which was all the more reason that she again told herself that any time she spent with him was time she *didn't* spend husband-hunting, and that she couldn't let herself be delayed any more than she already had.

"I'm sorry, but you're on your own from here," she repeated.

He returned to the chair beside her at the table where they'd been working, pulled it to face her rather than the computer and sat down, giving her a winning, alluring smile as his focus suddenly centered on her.

"You're right, you *have* accommodated me," he said. "You've gone above and beyond the call of duty and I'm grateful for that. But now I need insider information. I need to find people who were around a long, long time ago who might be able to help, and I don't think there's anyone more perfect than you are for figuring out who those people might be and introducing me to them."

Kate laughed and shook her head. "I see right through that schmoozing, and it isn't going to work. I have other things to do that I haven't been able to do for two nights now."

"Those *things* again. Are they as important as helping an old lady resolve a past that's making her miserable?"

"They're important to me. To my *future*."

The frown reappeared. "I thought we were talking about doing laundry or dusting or something. But that can't be important to your *future*. What exactly am I keeping you from?" he asked as if she'd intrigued him.

But she wasn't going to explain herself. "Just *things* that I need to get on with and can't do if I'm tied up with you."

The wicked smile slowly spread across his handsome face—as she'd known it would the minute that phrase had slipped out. And true to form, he couldn't let it go without saying, "Is being *tied up* with me such a horrible thing? Because I *can* make it worth your while...."

Kate stood her ground. "Being *tied up* with you is just not getting me where I need to be."

"Either housekeeping is *waaay* too big a deal to you or you have something else going on that you're not telling me."

"I have a lot going on that I'm not telling you. But the point is, I don't have time to just drop everything *I* have going on for what *you* have going on. Which I've done for two nights, now, and am not going to do anymore."

"How can I sweeten the deal to talk you into it?" he asked in a deeper tone than his normal voice, a more intimate tone that seduced.

But Kate ignored that, too, knowing he was just working her. "The most I will do from here is this—I'm going to visit my grandmother tomorrow night. She and the Reverend moved here right about the time Theresa would have left, so that would have been at the height of gossip about a baby suddenly appearing—if there was any. I'll talk to Celeste—"

"You call your grandfather *the Reverend,* and your grandmother *Celeste?*"

"I'm just getting to know her but that's a whole other

story. Anyway, I'll see what Celeste has to say. If she knows anything, I'll arrange for you to talk to her. If she can think of someone more likely to know something, I'll let you know and you can contact them."

"Why not just take me with you tomorrow night? That seems like some*thing* you have to do that I could just do with you."

Why not just bring him along? Because that would be the third evening she spent with him. The fourth if she counted the wedding. And the fact that she was enjoying this back-and-forth, the fact that she'd even enjoyed going through records with him for the last several hours, was warning enough for her to put an end to it.

"Nope," she said decisively and without offering any other reason. "Tomorrow night I'm seeing my grandmother and you're not. But if you can't wait…" She typed at the computer and then printed out the files she'd brought up. "I'll give you a list of the names that appear on the 1950 census of Northbridge and on the current census—"

"We already compared census reports and can't tell if the baby showed up that way."

"No, I've included the ages so you can see who was an adult at the time. You can figure out who's still alive and that will give you a place to start if you want to just do some cold-calling—"

"Oh, come on!" he said with a disbelieving laugh. "You aren't really going to leave me hanging out to dry that way? *Cold calls?*"

"I believe the agreement for tonight was that you were bringing dinner and you left me *hanging out to dry* on that score, so—"

"Oh, you are wrong about *that!*"

"About how you said you were going to bring dinner so we could eat while we worked and you didn't?"

"Yes, I said that and didn't *bring* dinner, but that doesn't mean I just blew it off."

Kate answered only with a raise of her eyebrows because she believed otherwise.

Ry got to his feet again. "Okay, then, that's it for us here. Shut down that computer and—"

"Let me guess—this is where you make a big show of how you didn't forget and pretend that you had something planned. Remember, I can see through you," she said.

"I'm going to make you eat those words before I feed you dinner," he threatened. "Now shut down that computer, do whatever you have to do to close the office, get in your car and meet me at Home-Max in fifteen minutes."

"Fifteen minutes? That's not going to be enough time to make it look like you really did have something planned."

"Fifteen minutes, Miss Doubting Thomas," he repeated.

Kate took the papers that had the census names on them from the printer and held the sheets out to him.

Ry merely laughed, refusing it. "You can file those in the trash—you're going to owe me some insider help after tonight."

"Is that so?" she said skeptically.

"Yes, it is so," he countered smugly. Then he said, "Fifteen minutes," again and left her to do as she'd been told.

Which she did, still convinced that he was bluffing.

She'd seen this kind of thing too often with the Peter Pans—no follow-through. They made promises or bargains like this one that Ry had made tonight for dinner in exchange for her help. But, in her experience, they couldn't be counted on. Which was why it hadn't surprised her when Ry had shown up empty-handed.

But point out the shortcoming the way she had with Ry? That inspired the Big Bluff—which she'd also seen before. He was probably running down Main Street right at that moment hoping he could find one of Northbridge's few restaurants still open so he could order some quick takeout and pretend it was what he'd planned.

But she'd play along, Kate decided. Just to see how far he could go in those fifteen minutes to try to pull something out of his hat before ultimately admitting he'd forgotten all about dinner.

It would be good for her.

Because the way Ry looked, all his charm, his humor, made it difficult for her to resist the attraction she had for him. The attraction she kept trying to deny she had for him. And had anyway.

But anything that gave concrete support to her contention that he was all fun and no future was good for her.

Because if anything could help dampen his appeal, it was that.

"Say it—say you underestimated me, that you were wrong."

"You didn't *bring* dinner to eat while we went through the records—that was what you said you were doing and you didn't," Kate contended as she stood in the middle of the under-construction Home-Max store where one spot had been cleared to set up a makeshift table.

"But I *didn't* forget. I'm good to my word and I've provided you with dinner. The best barbecue Missoula has to offer."

"They have a very widespread delivery area," Kate said.

"They didn't deliver it. I called the restaurant last night, got them to pack what I wanted, had the trucker driving in today pick it up, and since the trucker's wife was riding along this time, she did this setup for me."

This setup was a piece of plywood balanced on tile boxes to form a table that was covered with a linen tablecloth. There were also two packing crates turned on their sides for chairs. The table was set with paper plates, plastic forks, knives and spoons and an abundance of napkins, and in the center there were even lit candles on either side of a small arrangement of wildflowers.

It was all sweet and romantic and Kate liked it more than she wanted to, and she was hiding that fact behind maintaining that Ry had somehow dropped the ball. Because feeble though it was at that point, she knew that plays like this one were how she'd historically been sucked into lowering her guard with men who had ended up wrong for her, and she knew she just couldn't let it happen again.

"So, say you misjudged me," Ry demanded.

But that was the problem, she didn't think she had.

"In this—alone—I was mistaken," Kate admitted.

Ry laughed wryly. "Boy, you are a tough nut to crack, aren't you?"

"I am now," she said more under her breath than to him. To him, she said, "What's on the menu?"

"Crow, for you."

Kate laughed. "Yuck, barbecued crow? That doesn't sound good. Or is that tonight's delicacy to be slipped between the bars of my cage?" she asked, referring to his comment the evening before.

"I'm not broadening your horizons tonight, I'm just feeding you the best barbecue there is. A sauce that's a little sweet, a little smoky, a little tangy, a little spicy—that has it all—slathered on meat that's smoked in-house at this place and is so great you're gonna eat it and beg me for more."

"In your dreams, Grayson," Kate countered in response to another of his double entendres, inciting a surprised chuckle from him.

"Yeah, I'm trying not to have those dreams," he muttered himself this time. Then he motioned for her to sit down and said, "I don't know about you, but I'm starving."

Kate took one of the crate seats as Ry sat across from her.

"Bib?" he offered, holding out a white plastic adult-sized bib emblazoned with the restaurant's logo.

"No, thank you," she said, although she knew she probably should have accepted it. She'd given in to the urge to dress up more than she usually did for work today—low-riding black slacks, the most expensive white blouse she owned and a black pin-striped vest that she wore buttoned because then the U-neckline swooped just below her breasts and gave them a little boost. If she ruined that blouse with barbecue sauce she was going to shoot herself, but she just couldn't put a bib over it.

The sides of her hair were pulled to the top of her head and caught there with a comb but she'd left the rest to fall around her shoulders, and as she leaned forward to smell the food that Ry was uncovering she swept it back so it didn't get into anything.

"I don't know..." she said then, as if the aromas that were wafting to her weren't as good as they were. "North-bridge runs a barbecue cook-off every August that brings people from all around to compete. I've had some hard-to-beat barbecue."

"I think this can hold its own," he said confidently as he dished out pulled pork, beef brisket and smoked chicken and turkey so she could taste some of everything. Then he added a roll, potato salad and baked beans to her plate.

"You can make a sandwich, or eat the meat and the bread separately, or however you like it," he said after setting the dish in front of her and beginning to fill his own.

It required only a few bites before Kate had to admit that he was right—it was some of the best barbecue she'd ever eaten. And rather than the smugness she'd thought that would elicit from him when she told him so, he just seemed glad to have pleased her.

As they settled into eating, Kate glanced around and said, "Looks like Noah has been coming along on this. I know he's been working hard to knock down the walls so you'd have one big, open space."

"His crew should finish up this week. The truck that came in today brought shelving and racks and some initial supplies so we can get that phase started as soon as construction is complete."

"*We*—meaning you, Wyatt and Marti? Noah said the three of you run the whole Home-Max chain together. Is that right?"

"It's our baby," Ry confirmed. "Our grandfather opened the first hardware store—G and H Hardware. The H was for Hobbs because some of the launch-money came from Gram—we're figuring it's what she got from Tyson for her land. Our father took over when Gramps died. Dad branched out, opening a few more stores. Wyatt, Marti and

I got into it as teenagers as an after-school and weekend job. None of us worked through college—"

"Which Marti told me you did in record time," Kate said.

He shrugged. "I've always had a lot of energy, so yeah, I got my degree in three and a half years. And once we'd all graduated, the family business is what we went back to."

"Did you go to work ahead of Wyatt and Marti?"

Ry finished a bite of potato salad, shaking his head as he did. Then he said, "No, I went to Australia."

"Australia?"

"I wanted a little adventure and Australia seemed like the place for that. It was far away from home and a little on the rough-and-tumble side of things. I went to surf and scuba dive. I did some rowing and mountain biking. I went fly-fishing, hang gliding, rock climbing. I did some parachuting and I even entered a canoe race—it was great."

"It doesn't sound like a rest-and-relaxation kind of trip."

"Those kind of trips bore me to death."

Kate wasn't shocked by that news. "I don't like lying-around vacations, either. I like to have sightseeing and activities planned when I travel, but rock climbing and hang gliding?"

"Don't knock it until you've tried it."

"I'll pass, thanks. That kind of thing isn't for me—one of those differences between us, remember?"

Ry conceded to that with a shrug of his eyebrows.

"And when your Australian adventure was over," Kate went on, "did you come back and go to work?"

"I did. I stayed in Australia until Marti and Wyatt had finished their last semester of college, came back to do the whole formal graduation ceremony with them, and then we started in with G and H—doing more than clerking and stocking shelves the way we had before college. Dad eased us into running the whole shebang."

"And it's just grown from there?"

"Not quite. Unfortunately, when we lost our parents eight years ago, the whole shebang was floundering. The big home-improvement stores had come in and they were killing us. We were having to close one store after another until it was clear that we had to either give up the business entirely or make a change."

"I'm a little surprised that you didn't want to give up the business entirely and move on to something more exciting," Kate said. She'd eaten her fill by then and she pushed her plate away.

Ry saw that she was finished and took another container from a box near his chair, uncovering a dish of enormous chocolate chocolate chip cookies studded with pecans. "Also the best," he said as he set the dish nearer to Kate than to himself.

Kate could never resist chocolate and although she knew she should at least break one of the saucer-sized delicacies in half, she took a whole one.

"Good, huh?" Ry asked after she'd had a bite.

"Better if it was heated so the chocolate chunks were melty."

"That's exactly how I eat them at home—I put them in the toaster oven so they stay crisp on the outside and get warm and gooey on the inside," he said as if she'd read his mind. "But even cold they're still good."

He took a cookie of his own then and resumed talking about the family business.

"I don't know about *excitement,* but I like this business and while we considered giving it up entirely, that didn't seem like the best thing to do for any of us—including Gram, who's a silent partner. Marti, Wyatt and I didn't want to go our separate ways and Gram's care is expensive—letting her investment basically die wasn't going to do her any good, and we were afraid if we all just got jobs doing who knew what, we wouldn't be able to swing full-time, live-in nursing for her. So we decided to shake things up, make some changes and try to compete. We expanded from the hardware-only business to a full-scale home-improvement store and changed the name to Home-Max to get the word out. It was a gamble we took for all our sakes."

"But it paid off."

"We're doing okay," he said, understating the success Kate knew the chain had become.

She'd finished her entire cookie and was eyeing a second.

"Go ahead," Ry coaxed, apparently seeing her longing gaze at the dish. "I won't tell."

"Maybe just another half…" she said, breaking a second cookie in two pieces because she could never resist chocolate.

Still, as she savored more cookie, she said, "So you and Wyatt and Marti working together—you like that? You all get along?"

"Yes to both—we like it and you could count the number of problems we've had on one hand."

"Do you think that's because you're triplets? That you're more in tune with each other?"

He shrugged his shoulders this time. "We've always been close—probably that's the triplet thing. But whatever the reason, we balance each other out. Wyatt is the most down-to-earth, serious one of us. He's practical and logical and our bottom-line guy. Marti brings a lighter touch to things, and she's a great diplomat so she's good at taking all the perspectives and blending them, finding a way that makes us all happy."

"And you?" Kate asked, wondering how he categorized himself.

"I'm the impulsive one, the risk-taker. It was my suggestion that we pull out all the stops to compete with the big home-improvement guys, that we think on their level, even though it meant risking everything—*losing* everything if we didn't make it. It's usually me who lobbies for pushing the envelope."

"And Marti and Wyatt have to rein you in," Kate guessed.

"Sometimes. Sometimes they get onboard. Pushing the envelope, being impulsive, going with the flow, following your instincts—those aren't *always* bad things, you know?"

Kate knew that he was sending her a veiled message that maybe she should cut loose, too.

Her only response was a knowing, "Uh-huh."

That made him smile and nod at the second cookie she was about to finish since, somewhere along the way, she'd reached for the other half, too.

"Not always bad to step outside of the box and just go for it," he reiterated pointedly.

"Last night it was a cage, tonight it's a box—you should make up your mind," Kate counseled.

"All I know," he said with more intensity than she'd yet seen from him, "is that I watch my grandmother be afraid of her shadow—and of everything else real and imagined. I watch her and her illness keep her locked up tight. And it's not to anybody's benefit—least of all hers. It's made me *want* to push the envelope, and always, always stretch my wings as far as they'll go. It's made me want to try everything there is to try, and live the hell out of my life rather than *ever* give it over to that."

"So you've put some thought into it and it's kind of a goal that you have," Kate mused, interested to learn that. It didn't make him any less wrong for someone like her who wanted to settle down and live a quiet, small town life raising kids, but she at least had a slightly better understanding of what made him tick.

Thinking these thoughts, she stood up from the table before she gave in to a third jumbo cookie and spending more time with this man she was coming to like in spite of herself.

"It's late, I should get home," she said, grasping her paper plate to clean up.

Ry reached across the makeshift table and stopped her by putting one of his hands on one of hers. "I'll take care of this. I have work to do around here for another couple of hours anyway."

His hand was big and strong and warm and slightly callused. And for a moment, the feel of it covering hers was the only thing Kate could think about. *Liking* the feel of it covering hers was the only thing she could think about.

But that would never do, so she let go of her plate, pulling her hand out of his as she did. "Okay, then I'll leave it to you," she agreed in a voice that was softer than it should have been.

Ry stood, too. "I'll walk you out," he offered.

Kate could have protested. She probably should have. But she was still a little lost from the touch of his hand, so she just went to the door she'd come in and stepped out into the cooler night air.

Ry went with her to her car door, opening it for her.

But before she could get in he said, "So, what do you say? You owe me some insider help now, don't you think?"

Kate took a moment to recall that he wanted her help finding someone who knew about the possibility that his grandmother had delivered a baby long ago and what might have happened to it. That because she'd falsely accused him of forgetting to bring dinner, he wanted her help as payback.

But standing in the lee of her car door, Kate merely raised a serene smile to him. "I told you, I'll talk to Celeste tomorrow night and let you know what she has to say."

He sighed and shook his head at her, but there was a small smile on his handsome face, too, as he looked into her eyes in the light of the streetlamp.

But just when Kate expected more cajoling and coaxing, that wasn't what he did.

What he did was lean over the door to press his mouth to hers. Only for a moment. Stealing a kiss instead.

And then it was over so quick she hadn't even had the chance to react or kiss him back—not that she'd wanted to.

"I thought I wasn't your type?" she said, raising her chin to him as if even that slight buss hadn't added to the earlier touch of his hand to make her knees go just a little wobbly.

"Yeah…I keep telling myself that," he said in an almost-whisper.

But that was his only answer as he backed up a few steps.

Then he said, "I'll be waiting to hear what your grandmother has to say."

Kate merely nodded and got behind the wheel of her car, pulling the door closed.

But through the windshield she could still see Ry, standing on the curb in front of her car, watching her.

And all she could do as she backed up her car was think that, if he was going to kiss her, she wished he would have kissed her for real.

Chapter Five

Kate's grandmother lived in an apartment above the dry cleaners', where she'd worked for decades for the Pratt family. The dry cleaners' was in a storefront on Main Street but to get to the apartment required walking around to the alley where there was a rear door that accommodated the business and wooden steps that led up to the apartment.

When Kate arrived as planned at seven on Wednesday evening, the last thing she expected to find was Ry, leaning against the building wall between the dry cleaners' back door and the bottom of those stairs.

He had on a crisp white shirt with the sleeves rolled up to his elbows and a pair of jeans whose pockets provided slings for the thumbs that were hooked into them. One knee was bent so his cowboy-booted foot could be flat against the wall behind him. Cocky and sure of himself and aggravating and appealing all at once.

Kate was miffed that he'd ignored her refusal to bring him with her to see Celeste and came anyway.

Kate was also unreasonably elated to find him there.

She tried to deny the elation by ignoring it and put her energy into being miffed.

"What are you doing here?" she challenged.

He just smiled and said, "Intruding."

"Well, at least you're honest."

"To a fault," he confirmed. Then he nodded in the direction of the upstairs apartment and said, "I did some talking to the construction crew today. An interesting story that I hadn't heard before goes with this lady. Are you ashamed of her? Is that why you wouldn't bring me along?"

"No," Kate contended. She glanced nervously up at the apartment, fearing that a window might be open to let in the June air and that Celeste could have heard what he'd said even though he'd said it quietly—probably with the same thought in mind.

"Did it ever occur to you that I didn't want to bring you along just because I didn't want to bring you along?" she asked.

"Sure."

"But what you wanted was more important."

"Sure," he repeated matter-of-factly. "It's more important to me."

"So here you are, trying to get your own way." She wanted to sound angry and outraged. Why was it coming out more a petulantly flirtatious reprimand? As if she didn't actually mind that he was pushing himself into the situation?

"I'm not really trying to get my own way," he said then. "If I was, I would have gone up ahead of you and talked to Celeste myself—I did meet her at Wyatt's wedding and say hello to her again at Marti's, so it isn't as if she doesn't know who I am."

"Then what are you doing here?" she asked again, pushing back the thought that he was merely there to see her.

"I had another idea and it seemed as if your grandmother might be able to help with it even if she doesn't know anything about the mystery appearance of a baby around here fifty years ago. But I waited for you so that if you're still dead set against me tagging along, I'll just tell you what I thought of and have you add it to what you were going to ask her in the first place."

"You could have just called me," Kate pointed out.

He grinned. "I was also thinking that if you still don't want me to go with you, I could wait around until your visit is over, maybe buy you an ice cream cone?"

Again, was that so he could be with her or so he could immediately have whatever answers Celeste might give?

Kate knew she should believe it was so he could get his answers immediately.

But there was a part of her that *wanted* to believe the other.

"I don't like being steamrolled," she said.

"Yeah, that *would* melt the ice cream," he agreed amiably.

Kate did what she hoped was glare at him, at the same time she was actually appreciating the sight of his sculpted features and those piercing metallic blue eyes looking at her without any repentance whatsoever.

"Honestly, I'm not steamrolling you," he said after a moment. "I'm here to give you another question to ask your grandmother, and hang around until you come back down so that maybe we can walk to the ice cream shop and have a cone or a sundae, or whatever your heart desires. Information as quick as I can get it, and some entertainment and diversion where I can find it around this place—that's all I'm after."

So it was about him.

She saw that as a warning—the first and only thought the other men in her life had almost always had was about themselves. And what she was looking for was a man who *wanted* to be with her for her, not someone who was with her as an afterthought or because he didn't have anything better to do.

"I don't know about the ice cream," she said, realizing that she sounded defensive now. But protecting herself and her own goals was what she had to do. "But since you're here anyway, I suppose you might as well come up with me and ask your own questions. Then you'll have your answers as soon as I do."

He smiled but she knew he'd heard the change in her tone because he also looked slightly confused. "I don't have to go up. It's a nice night. I'm fine waiting here. And don't feel as if you even need to cut your visit short," he said, apparently assuming that going with her to see Celeste was what had set her off.

"It's fine," Kate said curtly.

He studied her for a moment, frowning at her.

Then he said, "The truth is, I spent all day thinking about how if I didn't do this tonight, I wasn't going to see you at all today, and I just couldn't get past that. I mean, I *did* think of something else to have you ask your grandmother, but you're right, I *could* have called. But then I only would have *talked* to you, I wouldn't have *seen* you."

Was he just saying that because he'd ticked her off? Or did he mean it?

She told herself she had to stop this second-guessing. That none of his motives should matter to her.

But what he said about wanting to see her was causing her to involuntarily slip back into that elation she'd felt when she'd first found him in the alley.

"Let's just go upstairs, visit with Celeste and then we'll see," she said.

"*We'll see*—better than nothing," he answered. "And maybe later you'll tell me why you call your grandmother Celeste and fill me in on the details of her notorious past."

"Maybe," Kate said, the flirtatiousness back, too, even though she hadn't intended for it to be.

Ry pushed off the wall and motioned for her to go up the steps ahead of him. Kate did, wishing she'd worn her butt-hugging jeans rather than her baggy ones, that the plain gray short-sleeved shirt she was wearing over a white T-shirt fit a bit more snuggly, too, and that she hadn't merely put her hair into a ponytail tonight.

But there was nothing she could do about it all and so when she reached the top landing, she merely knocked on the door as Ry joined her, standing closely enough behind her to send a whiff of his cologne her way, letting her know that he'd shaved before ambushing her and obviously put some thought into the fact that he would be seeing her.

Celeste answered the door within seconds. It led Kate to think she'd been nearby when Kate knocked because Celeste was a very rotund woman and didn't move with any speed.

"Kate! I'm so glad you came!" the elderly woman greeted her before glancing beyond her to Ry. "And...Ry, isn't it? You're Marti and Wyatt's brother."

Ry confirmed that he was and after exchanging hellos, Kate said, "I know you probably thought I was coming alone but—"

"Oh, it doesn't matter. The more the merrier," Celeste

assured them. "After so many years with so few people in my life, I'm thrilled to have all the visitors I can get now. Come in, come in and sit down. I'm hoping for some drinking advice—one of my bingo friends went on a cruise to Greece and brought me a bottle of ouzo. I've never had it before and don't know how to drink it. Maybe between the two of you, you can tell me."

"We're hoping you can help us out, too," Ry said from behind Kate as she went in and he brought up the rear.

Inside, Celeste made her way ponderously to the tiny kitchen on the other side of a half wall that separated it from the living room. Then she returned with an unopened bottle of the liqueur and three small glasses.

"Are you supposed to drink this fast—in a shot? Or sip it? Do you put it over ice or mix it with something?"

Setting the bottle and the glasses on the table in the corner of the L-shape formed by an easy chair and an old sofa, Celeste did a sort of a tumble backward into the easy chair.

"I don't know anything about ouzo," Kate said, moving to the sofa to sit down. "I know it's some kind of Greek drink but I've never had it. Have you?" she asked Ry.

"Many times," he answered with fondness. He went to the bottle and picked it up to look at the label. "I love Greece and all things Greek—including ouzo. Do you like licorice?" he asked Celeste.

"I do," she said as if it were a revelation.

"Then you'll probably like ouzo. I've seen it slammed back in shots, but I like to drink it slowly, mixed with a little water, talking with friends—that's how I've always had it in Greece. But this is one of the most potent versions—over forty percent alcohol. We could get very drunk on this even *with* water to dilute it."

Kate saw him smile and wink at her grandmother. She saw Celeste's delight even before the elderly woman said, "But if it's a drink to have talking with friends then this seems like just the right time to open it and try it—with friends and family."

"None for me, thanks," Kate said.

Both her grandmother and Ry voiced their disappointment and tried to cajole her out of her refusal.

"I don't like licorice," she insisted.

"Then you'll have to have something else," Celeste said. "Wine or whiskey or—"

"Water—I'll have a glass of that while the two of you try the ouzo. I'll even bring water for your ouzo," Kate announced, getting up to do as she'd promised.

Ry cast her a look that said she'd disappointed him, but he didn't pressure her. He merely opened the bottle as she went to the kitchen. He'd poured some of the ouzo into two of the glasses by the time Kate rejoined them with a tumbler full of water for herself and another for Ry to douse the liqueur with.

"So you've been to Greece?" Celeste asked Ry when he handed one of the diluted ouzos to her.

"I have," he said before advising, "Just sip it." Then he took his own drink with him to sit on the sofa not far from the spot Kate had returned to and expanded on his answer. "I've been to Greece three times—twice during trips that included other countries in Europe, too, so I was only there for a few days both of those times. But the third time, I spent nearly a whole summer living there."

"Tell us about it," Celeste encouraged enthusiastically.

It didn't surprise Kate that her newfound grandmother wanted to hear about traveling to faraway places. Restlessness in her younger years was partly responsible for the bad turn Celeste's life had taken and her absence from Kate's life when she was growing up. But hearing about someone else's adventures obviously gave her a little vicarious pleasure even now and Kate didn't mind.

Ry was an energetic storyteller and without imbibing the ouzo the other two were drinking, Kate hung on every word of his descriptions and anecdotes, secretly appreciating the chance to just watch him, too. Enjoying that as much as what he was saying.

As the evening progressed, Kate and her grandmother plied him with questions, and Kate was as much to blame as Celeste was for getting Ry to go on and on as if he were giving a travel lecture. But as summer darkness finally began to dim the room to announce just how late it was getting, Ry said, "Okay, enough about this. Before I get you too drunk, Celeste, I need some information."

"Anything," the elderly woman said, clearly smitten with the charming Ry by then—no doubt aided by the fact that they'd both also had two glasses of ouzo.

Kate again only listened as he explained the Graysons' theory that Theresa had had a baby, that they were wondering if Celeste might know anything about that or have heard any gossip about a family mysteriously growing all those years ago.

"I wish I could tell you something useful," Celeste responded when he was finished. "But your grandmother had already left town when my family got here. I did hear some talk about Hector misusing a young girl's trust in him to get all that land, but I never heard anything about a baby. Or anything about anyone in Northbridge getting one under questionable circumstances."

"But you had another thought, too, you said," Kate reminded Ry with only a hint of challenge to her tone.

He smiled a private smile at her and muttered, "Suspicious to the end," before he refocused on Celeste and said, "It occurred to me today that if there *was* a baby, someone other than Tyson or his wife could have delivered it. If you know who the doctor was here at the time and he's still around, maybe we could coax some answers out of him."

"Northbridge didn't have its own resident doctor when we first moved here," Celeste said. "A doctor from Billings came in one day a week—unless there was a blizzard and then we could go even longer without seeing him. What we did have was a nurse who also performed as a midwife—she would have been more likely to deliver any baby born then. And I would think if it was some kind of secret, Hector wouldn't have wanted an out-of-town doctor in on it anyway. He's always been like Armand—"

"*Armand* is my grandfather—the Reverend," Kate filled Ry in.

"Yes, the Reverend," Celeste confirmed. "Well, like Armand, Hector's power tends to be the strongest within our city limits. Outside of Northbridge I suppose Hector could pay for what he wants, but I'm not sure that's always as effective as the kind of intimidation he practices here."

"Who was the midwife then?" Kate asked.

"She's yours, Kate," Celeste said. "Fiona."

"*Yours?*" Ry asked of Kate.

But it was Celeste who answered, "Our Adopt-A-Senior program—some of the young people take on the job of looking after the older folks who don't have family left. Kate takes care of Fiona. Fiona Templeton."

"But Fiona couldn't have been the midwife," Kate said,

thinking that her grandmother must be confused. "Fiona talks all the time about the Templetons coming to Northbridge in 1960."

"Bill Templeton and his brother John. But Fiona was Fiona Briggs before that and she had been here years already when I got to Northbridge. She'd come in the late 1940s to take care of an aunt and decided to stay."

"I didn't know that," Kate said. "From listening to Fiona, I just assumed she'd been a Templeton when she'd arrived—in 1960 with the rest of the Templetons." Kate hadn't even glanced at the census printouts she'd handed over to Ry the evening before or Fiona's first name might have clicked. "So Fiona married and had her son much later in her life than I thought," Kate said then.

Celeste did the math. "She had to have been at least thirty-nine when she married. I know she was in a hurry to find a husband and have a baby before it got any later for her. So see, Kate, you still have lots of time."

That comment brought a quizzical glance from Ry but Kate merely did a scant shake of her head as if she didn't know what her grandmother was talking about.

Then Celeste saved her by getting back to the subject. "Anyhow, if it's the midwife all those years ago who you want to talk to, that would be Fiona. She did that until we got our own doctor—that was just before I left town. By the time I slinked back, she'd quit being a nurse to stay home with her son."

"Her son was born with a lot of health problems. He passed away on his twenty-first birthday," Kate explained to Ry as if he would want to know, when, in fact, she was just trying to keep the ball rolling away from Celeste's remark about her still having time to get married and have kids.

Then Celeste said to Ry, "So you have an in when it comes to talking to Fiona—Kate can bring you along when she visits her. She goes almost every day."

"Really…" Ry said, drawing the word out and smiling mischievously at Kate. "Do you hear that? Your grandmother says you have to bring me with you to see this Fiona."

"I don't *have* to do anything," Kate countered.

"Oh, you sounded so much like your grandfather just then!" Celeste said, somewhat tipsy and just a little horrified.

"Tell her, Celeste," Ry urged. "Tell her that she doesn't have a choice—she *has* to take me to talk to Fiona."

"I don't know why she wouldn't," Celeste said as if Kate must have only been joking. "She'll be going, she might as well bring you along."

Chapter Six

"So, if I ever want to get you to leave in a hurry now I know how to do it—compare you to the Reverend and the tides turn," Ry mused as he and Kate sat at one of the wrought-iron bistro tables outside the ice cream parlor.

They'd left Celeste just shortly before and walked to the corner of Main and South, arriving at the ice cream shop when it was on the verge of closing. Kate had persuaded the teenager who was running the place to serve two more cones and then Kate—with her single scoop—and Ry—with his double—had gone outside to eat them.

"It was nearly nine o'clock," Kate reasoned in response to Ry's remark that the comparison to her grandfather had caused her to end their evening with Celeste. "And I decided I *did* want ice cream. We needed to get here before they closed. It didn't have anything to do with Celeste saying I reminded her of the Reverend."

"Uh-huh," Ry said, denying her rationalization. "You didn't like that *at all*."

Kate shrugged as if he were making a bigger deal out of it than it was. "Who *would* want to be compared to my grandfather? He's stuffy and eternally indignant and judgmental and demanding and heavy-handed. Would *you* want to be compared to him?"

"No!"

"I rest my case."

Ry smiled in the midst of finishing his top scoop. "I like Celeste, though," he said. "But from what I was told today, she left the Reverend—and her two sons—and ran off with a bank robber? Can that be true?"

"It's true. Although technically, the story goes that she changed her mind when she found out the man and his partner had robbed the bank. But he forced her to go with him anyway, after killing his partner in a fight over Celeste and burying him in the woods," Kate explained.

"It sounded too fantastic to believe when the electrician said it this morning," Ry marveled.

"Celeste says that it was a matter of falling in love with the wrong man at a time when she just couldn't take the Reverend's iron-fisted rule and being his more-than-perfect wife and the pillar of the community anymore."

"So she cut loose. And you don't approve," Ry guessed.

"I don't approve or disapprove. I can understand how my grandfather would drive any woman away. But to leave her kids behind? At the mercy of the man she couldn't stand to be around? I can't say that's something I admire."

"So you call her Celeste rather than anything more familiar."

"I call her Celeste because I've only actually known

who she is for a couple of months," Kate said, getting down to the chocolate-lined cone—her favorite part.

"How can that be? I was under the impression that she'd been a fixture in Northbridge for decades," Ry said.

"She has been. She's been Leslie, the clerk at the dry cleaners'."

Ry frowned at her, letting her know he was still confused, so Kate explained that, too.

"The bank robber took her to Alaska where he abandoned her, penniless. By then it was a case of kidnapping and she regretted leaving my dad and uncle, but she was afraid no one would believe either of those things. She decided that she at least wanted to be in the proximity of her sons, but in order to get from Alaska to Montana, she had to take whatever jobs she could, save up, and essentially do it inch by inch."

"That couldn't have been easy."

"It took her years, and over those years she put on so much weight that she didn't look anything like she had. She was living outside of town but when she realized there was such a change in her appearance, she took a chance and ventured into Northbridge again. No one recognized her. So she gave herself a phony name, and took the job at the dry cleaners' in order to at least be able to see my father and my uncle from a distance again."

"She fooled even the Reverend?"

"No, actually, he did figure it out at some point, but he used her fear that she could be blamed for the bank robbery against her, to keep her out of my dad's and my uncle's lives. He liked that she could only know her own family from afar—it was his retribution. She's kept tabs on everyone, with none of us having any idea who she really was."

"And how did this finally come out?" Ry asked, getting to the cone portion of his treat, too.

"A few months ago, when restorations on the north bridge—"

"Is that what the town is named for?" Ry interrupted her to ask.

"Yes. When restorations started on the bridge, the old bank bags were discovered along with the belongings of one of the robbers—until then it was believed that both robbers had gotten away. That reopened the old crime, which led to finding the remains of the second robber, and ultimately revealed that Leslie from the dry cleaners' was really Celeste. Our long-lost grandmother."

"And so now you're trying to get to know her on a different level—not as just the clerk at the dry cleaners'."

"We all want to have some sort of relationship with her, yes. My sister Meg and my brothers and our cousins are putting effort into that. None of us want to just ignore the fact that she's our grandmother, even if we didn't grow up aware of that."

Unlike Kate, Ry tired of his cone before he'd finished it and threw it into a nearby trash receptacle. It was a small thing—that simple toss of half a wafer cone a foot or two away—and yet there was something indescribably sexy about it.

Then he compounded the effect by drawing that now-free hand through his hair—long, thick fingers, a palm big enough to cup a basketball, carelessly dragged through those sun-streaked strands to unwittingly muss it to divine masculine perfection.

Kate took a sip of water as if she needed to wash down

the last of her cone. It was actually the sight of Ry—and her appreciation of it—that she was trying to swallow.

"I was introduced to Celeste—along with everybody else—at the weddings," Ry said then. "But nobody told me anything except that she was Noah's grandmother and a close friend of Neily's and the rest of the Pratts. I could tell there was some weirdness but I thought that was just because she and your grandfather were divorced," Ry said. "This is a lot more interesting."

"And a little embarrassing," Kate said under her breath.

"Now *that's* something I'd expect to hear from the Reverend." The grin that went with that was mischievous.

"Just a little embarrassment was not the Reverend's reaction."

"What about the rest of your family? Are they embarrassed by Celeste?"

"Everyone feels differently. None of us holds it against her. We've all lived under the tyranny and dictates of the Reverend and, I guarantee you, it was no fun. His effects can be tracked through all of us."

"In what way?"

"There was a lot of rebellion in one form or another. Noah got into some trouble as a teenager. Our oldest brother Jared kept a kind of hard shell around himself before he married Mara Pratt and actually let someone in." Kate shrugged. "It's just shaped who we all are to varying degrees."

"What about you? Did you rebel?"

Kate could see that Ry didn't believe she had. "I dated an inappropriate, forbidden boy," she said. "One of Noah's troublemaking friends, who's now in jail, as a matter of fact."

That made Ry grin again. "That *is* scandalous," he said as if it wasn't.

"I also wanted to marry him and ran away to be with him when his family moved out of Northbridge. We tried to elope, my parents had to send the police after us. It was kind of a mess."

And a pattern in the years since, she thought then—wanting to be married but choosing men who weren't going to get her there.

Seeming intrigued, Ry said, "You ran away from home, chasing after some teenage bad boy—"

"He was more than just a *bad boy*. Noah was that. Roland was a vandal and a thug. And, in the end, a thief who went to prison for robbing a store."

"So you chased after some guy who was a vandal, thug and thief, and tried to elope with him? That's a lot like what Celeste did, isn't it? Maybe you're more like her than the Reverend."

Kate chafed under that comparison, too. "I was sixteen, in the throes of teenage love and angst. I wasn't an adult with a husband or kids that I was leaving behind," she qualified.

"Still, you were in love with a not-so-upstanding guy and you ran off to be with him."

Put like that, there was no denying it.

"It *must* be genetic, then," Kate said facetiously.

Ry shrugged as if that was the only thing it could be.

But Kate wasn't letting that fly. "It wasn't genetic and I can assure you that what my grandmother had done *eons* before I was even born was not any influence, either. The more my family—particularly the Reverend—tried to force me to stay away from Roland, the more determined I was to be with him. The more determined I was to believe I was madly in love with him and destined to be with him. I convinced myself that I couldn't live without him, and if his parents were ripping us apart by moving, the only solution was for us to get married—like I said, teenage love and angst, and rebellion against a grandfather who preached virtue."

The boy who had been closing up the ice cream parlor came out then to tell them he had to bring the tables and chairs inside now.

Kate and Ry had no choice but to leave, and while Kate knew that was for the best, she was also aware of a reluctance to have the evening come to an end. Despite the fact that she hadn't set out to spend this evening with Ry in the first place.

Still, they began to retrace their steps along the sidewalk in front of Main Street's shops, heading for the dry cleaners' and Kate's car.

As they did, Ry picked up their conversation where they'd left off. "Are you telling me that you weren't virtuous at sixteen?" he asked, clearly liking that possibility.

"*Virtuous* by my grandfather's standards meant that I wasn't supposed to even *talk* to boys I wasn't related to."

Ry looked over at her and wiggled his eyebrows suggestively. "But surely you did more than talk with The Thug you were in love with."

"For your information, my virginity was still intact when the police dragged me back here. I hadn't done anything but kiss *The Thug*. Well, and a little under-the-shirt action," she confessed, wondering why she was telling Ry—of all people—*that*.

And why, at the same time, she was imagining a little under-the-shirt action with him.

But she curbed that thought in a hurry.

"So let me get this straight," Ry said then. "You were

rebelling in your choice of guys and in running away to be with him, but your puritanical side still prevailed because you were running away to *marry* him."

"I never thought about it like that, but I guess so," Kate confirmed.

They had walked very, very slowly without Kate being sure which of them had set the pace, but it still seemed as if they reached her car quicker than she wanted to.

"Do you need a ride home?" she asked when they were both standing by the hood, thinking that driving him to his grandmother's house would prolong this a little without seeming like she was trying to.

But it wasn't to be.

"Nah," Ry said. "My motorcycle is at the store. I walked over from there and I still have more work to do tonight, so that's where I'm headed."

Kate nodded and resigned herself to saying good-night.

But before she could, she glanced up to find Ry smiling slyly as he said, "What time are we going to see Fiona The Midwife tomorrow?"

Kate had no idea why his audacity made her smile in return.

Still, she sighed with mock disgruntledness.

"Your grandmother said you have to," he reminded before she'd said anything.

"I don't *have* to do anything," she repeated what she'd said earlier. But as with her rebukes of him in the alley, for some reason there was more coyness to her tone than she'd intended.

"But you will," Ry said, cocky and sure of himself again, too.

She knew there was no sense arguing with him. He was

going to win, one way or another—whether it be the argument or merely finding out where Fiona lived and showing up there like he had tonight with Celeste.

Besides, no matter how sure she was that she should say no and hold her ground and keep the biggest, thickest, highest wall between herself and Ry Grayson, she wasn't doing all that well at it.

Especially when, now that they were standing there under the light of the streetlamp at her car, the way they had been at the end of the previous evening, she was re-calling that brief nothing-of-a-kiss he'd given her and won-dering if she was going to get a second, better one. And that was where a whole lot more of her thoughts were centered than on arguing with him.

So she said, "I'm bringing Fiona dinner tomorrow. I usually sit with her while she eats—"

"You don't eat with her?"

"She likes to eat dinner at four in the afternoon. That's a little early for me."

"Four it is, then," Ry said. "Shall I meet you some-where or pick you up or what?"

"It's probably best if *I* pick *you* up." Because Kate had no intention of riding on his motorcycle. But she didn't want to say that.

"Okay," he agreed.

"Will you be at Home-Max then, too, or—"

"I'll go back to the house and shower first. How about picking me up there?"

"At a little before four—I can do that," Kate said.

"Great!"

And that was it. There was nothing left but to go their separate ways.

Yet Kate was looking up at him. And he was looking down at her. And while there hadn't been the slightest physical contact between them the entire evening, she was still thinking about last night's kiss.

And wondering if there would be another.

They were certainly in position for it, standing there without much distance between them.

But they shouldn't, she reminded herself. *She* shouldn't.

So why was she wishing she could?

She tipped her chin upward a little, getting an even better view of that handsome face glazed by the golden glow of the streetlamp. And it *was* handsome. Handsome enough for the image of it to have stayed with her all through the previous night, all through work today. Handsome enough for her to have stared at it the entire time he'd talked about Greece, to have etched it so thoroughly into her brain that she knew she wasn't likely to be free of the image tonight, either.

Tack on a second kiss to that, a kiss she might actually experience, a kiss that might leave her with a memory to add to the mental picture of him, and it would only make things worse, she told herself. It would only make him as hard to resist as chocolate.

"I should get going," she whispered without any eagerness whatsoever.

"Me too," he said, louder but in the same tone.

But neither of them moved.

Then Ry smiled as if something had just occurred to him. "I can't get over there being a side of you that was so impassioned that you ran away to elope with a thug."

"It was a long time ago."

"Too bad," he said as if that disappointed him the way her not drinking ouzo had.

One of Kate's eyebrows arched all on its own at that, challenging him to see just how impassioned she could still be even as she warned herself not to provoke anything.

Ry reached a hand to her upper arm, taking it in a firm but tender grip that felt so good it made her want to lean into him. Then his thumb rubbed up and down, under the short sleeve of her shirt and tiny shivers rippled from that spot.

He's going to do it again, he's going to kiss me.

Kate's chin went up another fraction of an inch. She felt her lips part just a bit.

She saw Ry come forward, but only slightly, still looking into her eyes.

Go ahead...do it.

Everything seemed to freeze as she waited for it. Waited for his mouth to come to hers. For him to sweep her off her feet with a kiss that would put that other one to shame.

But he didn't.

She had no idea why, but he didn't.

He gave her arm a squeeze and let go.

Taking a step backward, he jammed both hands into his back pockets and said, "I'll see you tomorrow."

"Okay," Kate answered, hearing the letdown in her own voice and hoping that he hadn't.

Even if he had, though, it didn't keep him from turning toward the new Home-Max store and leaving her standing there at the front end of her car, watching him.

So I guess I'm really not his type, she thought as an unexpected wave of dejection washed over her.

Not that it wasn't for the best that he hadn't kissed her. That she wasn't his type. Or so she told herself.

But regardless of how much she believed that, it didn't help.

Sighing a resigned—and intensely frustrated—sigh, she finally got into her car, started the engine and backed out of her parking spot.

Before she drove away, though, she took one last glance at Ry in her rearview mirror. He was just reaching the storefronts that would be Home-Max and rather than go in, he paused and looked in her direction, too.

Was he sorry he hadn't kissed her? As sorry as she was that he hadn't?

She wanted to think that he was.

But if he'd really wanted to do it, he probably would have. He was just that kind of guy.

Which meant that he must not have wanted to.

That didn't raise her spirits any.

Kate forced her eyes away from the mirror and pushed on the gas, getting herself out of there.

But even as she did she was wondering how many things were worse than going home unkissed when she'd been so sure she was going to be kissed.

And not just kissed.

For some reason, in all the thinking she'd done about Ry and that scant peck of Tuesday night, she'd just been sure that if he were to kiss her for real, it would be a kiss better than any kiss she'd ever had before.

Chapter Seven

"Here's your shirt, Ry."

"Thanks, Mary Pat. And thanks for ironing it for me," Ry said when his grandmother's caregiver brought him the black windowpane–checked shirt.

"Happy to do it. This is one of those custom-made Italian shirts you just got, isn't it?"

"It is," Ry confirmed, fighting the urge to explain why it had arrived by overnight mail today.

But Mary Pat didn't seem curious, she merely handed him the hanger and left. Leaving Ry grateful for not having to tell her that Kate was the reason he'd had his brother send him more clothes in a hurry. It seemed so damn adolescent to care as much as he did about the way he looked when he was going to see her that he didn't want to admit to it.

Besides, it was a little after three on Thursday afternoon

and he didn't have time to waste talking anyway. He needed to shower and shave before Kate picked him up to meet the former midwife.

He closed his bedroom door, hooked the hanger on the doorknob, and headed for the connected bathroom.

But Kate was still on his mind as he stripped down and stepped into the shower. Kate and his reaction to her.

He shouldn't have been having any reaction to her— that was the point. At least he shouldn't have been having any reaction to her beyond what he might have to any acquaintance.

It wasn't as if they were dating. They were only getting together so she could help him out—whether it was his shoulder massage or doing her job as city clerk or taking him to talk to people in the furtherance of his grandmother's cause. So worrying about what she might think of how he was dressed was dumb. Letting her get to him was just plain ridiculous.

And yet she *was* getting to him. She made him feel the way he had when he'd first noticed girls, he thought as he stood in the spray of steamy water. He was ultra-aware of even the smallest things about her, and ultra-self-conscious of even the smallest things about himself.

Just what he needed—puberty-part-two, he thought. But he wasn't sure what else to call it when he was torn between getting excited by something as simple as the way she raised her chin just before she was going to challenge him over something, and worrying if he'd remembered to put lotion on his hands so that they wouldn't be too rough just in case he got the chance to run his fingertips anywhere on that velvet skin.

Not that he'd gotten the chance to run his fingertips

anywhere at all on that velvet skin. But the thought of it did have him drifting in and out of fantasies.

Like right at that moment when he was still standing under the shower's spray, daydreaming instead of actually showering.

He grabbed the bar of soap and began to lather up with almost punishing strokes to snap himself out of his reverie.

Since he'd evolved out of adolescence, it usually took a lot to shake his cool with women. Not even women he really liked did it. But Kate Perry?

She did it.

And he wasn't sure why.

It was almost as if some sort of primitive urge had taken hold of him. Some kind of caveman thing, a primal imperative to be attractive to her, to woo her, to win her. And there was nothing he could do to curb it.

"But you need to," he advised himself when he replaced the soap in the dish and began to shampoo his hair with that same wake-up-you-idiot vehemence to bring home the point that, if anything, he should have fewer urges when it came to Kate.

He liked her—there was no denying it. But that didn't mean that anything else had changed. He was still convinced that she was too serious, too controlled, too conservative, too unadventurous for his taste. And that all spelled wet blanket to him.

No, that wasn't how he'd felt about her yet. But given time, it would happen. He was sure of it. Like last night when she hadn't even been willing to *try* the ouzo—yes, she'd laughed and been good company and seemed to have as much fun as he and Celeste had had. But still, it would have been nice if Kate would have just sipped the stuff, if only to experience it. He'd really wanted her to just do that much.

She probably would have done it when she was in that rebellious teenage phase she'd told him about later. When she'd believed she was in love and was determined to be with that guy who was in jail now.

Apparently once upon a time there had been a little fire to her. And Ry could just imagine her on her high horse, running away from home to get married.

The image made him chuckle.

But he *was* just imagining it. She'd relayed the story matter-of-factly and as if she had been talking about someone other than herself. Someone she didn't approve of. And that was what he needed to hang on to, he told himself. Because while there might have been some fervor to her a long time ago, she'd made sure he knew it *had* been a long time ago, that now she had that part of herself contained.

To have Kate full of fire and passion, though? That would be exactly how he'd want her. But he just didn't think that was who she was now.

He shook his head hard and flung shampoo in every direction before stepping under the shower's spray again to rinse off.

So, yes, Kate was wrong for him in the long run.

Did he have a history of denying himself a little short-run fun with a woman he knew was wrong for him?

Denying himself someone who had him this interested was not something he usually did, no.

But it was something he had to do this time. Kate was his sister's in-law and that cinched it. He had to keep the bigger picture in mind when it came to her so, no, there couldn't be any short-run fun, either.

Well, that wasn't exactly true because he *did* have fun when he was with her—that was part of the problem and why he kept *wanting* to be with her.

He just couldn't have any short-run, *messing-around* fun. He couldn't give in to his hormones and indulge those thoughts that she was the most beautiful thing he'd ever seen and that he wanted her to be his for a while—the way he could have if they really were fifteen and she'd come onto his radar.

But it wasn't any easier to ignore that inclination now than it would have been if he *had* been a hormonal teenager.

Because like any obsessed pubescent kid, he couldn't stop thinking about her. He was even dreaming about her. And yeah, he was overly concerned with what he was wearing and how his hair turned out and if his shave was close enough.

Close enough so his face would be smooth if he kissed her.

Like he had the night before last.

But he shouldn't have done that and he knew it. Kissing her was not keeping this on the right terms. Kissing her would take this outside of the safety zone and put more at risk. Which was why he hadn't kissed her again last night.

Even though he almost had.

Even though never before had not kissing someone tied him into such knots.

God, but he'd wanted to kiss her.

He finished rinsing and turned off the water, grabbing the towel he'd left over the top of the shower door, roughing himself up a little with that, too.

It didn't help. He still wanted to kiss her. Maybe if he'd just done it up better the first time that would have been enough to satisfy him.

Ooh, thinking *that* was a risky little gamble! That actually kissing her more thoroughly might be the antidote to the primal urges and imperatives? That it could turn him off and leave him impervious to everything about her that was getting under his skin more and more with each time he saw her?

He recognized what he was doing; he was finding a way around what he knew he shouldn't do. He was finding a way to give himself license to kiss her again.

But if he kissed her and liked it even more than he'd liked that single little peck, how would he stay in the safety zone then?

He probably wouldn't. He probably wouldn't be *able* to.

So it was a bad end-run idea.

A bad end-run idea that was taking him over more with every second it sat there in his brain.

"Don't do it—" he warned as if he were talking to someone else.

But then he finished drying off and went to the sink to shave.

Straight razor or electric?

A close enough shave to know he wouldn't scratch her or a not-so-close shave?

He knew what he *should* do—shave with the electric so maybe the thought of stubble would keep him in line.

Staying in line was what he needed to do. For everyone's sake.

"So electric it is," he decreed.

But somehow when he reached into the medicine cabinet, his hand went for the razor.

"Just pile it on."

At Ry's encouragement, Kate added a third cardboard

box to the top of the two he was already holding. "I hope these boxes are clean," she fretted.

"Don't worry about it."

They were standing beside Kate's car in Fiona Templeton's driveway at four o'clock Thursday afternoon. Ry had insisted that he carry in everything Kate had brought with her, so Kate was taking the boxes from her backseat and loading him up. But she *was* worried that the boxes she'd used to cart everything might soil the shirt they were resting against because it was a fabulous shirt that fitted him to perfection and she would hate to get it dirty.

"You must not come to see this lady too often," he said when she took several hangers of dry cleaning to carry herself.

"I come every other day, call every morning and almost every evening," Kate said. "But Fiona has horrible arthritis and can barely get around her house. She only goes out on Sunday to church—if it's a warm day. So I bring her groceries and her dry cleaning and books from the library and DVDs that I rent for her and whatever else she needs. Today I also have her old toaster because she insisted I have it repaired rather than replace it for her. Plus, on the days I visit, I make a lot of food for her so she gets more than one meal out of it. It all tends to add up. If it's too heavy for you—"

"I think I can handle it," he said. Then he smiled and asked hopefully, "Will she have ouzo like your grandmother did?"

Kate laughed. "Degenerate," she called him even as she appreciated the way his smile drew creases down his cheeks and put a few laugh lines at the corners of his remarkable eyes.

Then she added, "No, Fiona will not have ouzo. She's a strict teetotaler. She's also a no-nonsense kind of person so don't expect that flirting you did with my grandmother last night to work here."

"Guess I'll have to pull something else out of my bag of tricks," he said as if he were accepting a challenge.

Kate didn't doubt that he had a bag of tricks when it came to charm. But even if he didn't, he looked terrific enough to win just about anyone's good graces.

She couldn't be sure whether he did justice to the shirt or the shirt did justice to him. But either way, the fine fabric and the excellent cut accentuated his broad shoulders, hinted at bulging biceps inside of long sleeves that were rolled to his elbows, and skimmed his torso like a seductive whisper before being tucked into jeans that hugged his rear end in what seemed like an invitation to grab it.

Not that she wanted to.

Well, not that she would, even though she *might* want to.

But still, he looked great, he smelled great, and she thought that any woman of any age would be bowled over by him with just one glance.

Certainly she was....

Although she admitted to herself that the fact that he hadn't kissed her the night before had left her all the more preoccupied by him. She just couldn't stop wondering why he hadn't kissed her, if he found her unattractive or unappealing.

And even though she'd told herself a gazillion times that being unattractive to him made her life simpler, the possibility still gnawed at her.

So much so that she'd cut her workday short today to go home at noon in order to take a second shower, wash her hair and let it air-dry while she scrunched it repeatedly to put it at its shiniest, its fullest, its waviest.

So much so that she'd given herself a manicure and a pedicure, and taken special care when she'd applied her blush, mascara and lip gloss.

So much so that she'd changed her outfit three times before settling on a lacy camisole underneath a filmy white blouse that barely reached the waistband of a pair of gray capri pants that showed off the new sandals she'd been saving for a special occasion—ultimately dressing up more than she ever did just to visit Fiona. Dressing up for a man who hadn't wanted to kiss her last night.

But what *she* didn't want to do was think about that, so to distract herself as they headed for Fiona Templeton's small white stucco house, she said, "I've been wondering why you didn't just ask your grandmother who delivered her baby. We don't even know that it *was* Fiona."

"Gram's been in one of her bad funks. Neither Mary Pat nor I have been able to roust her out of bed for the last two days," he answered along the way. "When she gets like this, we have to just focus everything on trying to coax her to get up or even to eat. The last thing I should do is ask her something that might upset her more than she already is."

"I'm sorry," Kate said, afraid she might have sounded insensitive.

But he took her apology as empathy and said, "Yeah, me, too. It really gets to me when she's suffering worse than usual."

That last part had come out in a deeper, quieter voice. Kate had the distinct impression that he was confiding something to her that he didn't readily share with just anyone. And it touched her. And put a dent in the resolve she kept trying to wrap herself in.

"Maybe Fiona can tell us something that will help," she said to console him.

"Let's keep our fingers crossed."

They'd reached the front door. Kate rang the bell but didn't wait for it to be answered, just opened the door herself, calling as she did, "Fiona? It's me. And company."

Then she ushered Ry in, still curious to see how he handled the tough-as-nails Fiona.

And suddenly hoping the tough-as-nails Fiona didn't give him too hard a time.

"So the best we got out of that was that Fiona didn't approve of what went on in Tyson's house with *young Theresa*," Ry said as he and Kate left the old woman's house two and a half hours later.

"I'm sorry," Kate said as they got back into her car.

Asking the elderly Fiona about what she knew in regard to Theresa having had a baby by Hector Tyson fifty years ago had met with stonewalling from Fiona. Ry had taken it in stride but Kate felt bad about it.

"She liked you, though. She never lets anyone touch that grandfather clock and she let you set it."

"But when she digs in her heels and says she has nothing to say on the subject, she apparently means it," Ry said as Kate backed out of the driveway.

"Still, the disapproval thing—that implies that she was there, doesn't it?" Kate asked, trying to make the most out of the small amount Fiona had said. "And since she *was* the person who delivered babies then, and she didn't *deny* that your grandmother had a baby…"

"Yeah," Ry conceded, "it isn't anything concrete, by any means, but I'm taking it as a sort-of confirmation. Or at least as another step toward the likelihood that there was a baby. But did you see what she did when I pushed her to tell me what had happened to that baby? I've never seen a mouth pinch shut like that."

"I saw it," Kate said. "I guess she'd warned you that she wasn't going to say any more and she wasn't kidding."

"I can't imagine that woman ever kidding about anything."

Kate laughed again. He hadn't seemed daunted by Fiona but maybe he had been, just a little. And that tickled Kate even as she regretted that he hadn't gained any real ground for his grandmother.

"Could Tyson have some kind of hold over her that caused her to clam up?" he asked then.

"Over Fiona? You mean something that would make her afraid to tell you? Oh, I don't think so. I don't think Fiona would have ever let anyone have any kind of hold over her. I'd say this is more a matter of ethics—"

"Or self-protection if she had a hand in whatever happened to the baby and it wasn't on the up-and-up."

"Fiona would never do anything that wasn't on the up-and-up. Or even turn a blind eye to it if she knew someone else was. If she delivered a baby that belonged to your grandmother and Hector, she did it to help your grandmother regardless of her own feelings about the situation. And if there was a baby, and if she knew what was going to happen to that baby, it wasn't anything awful because she would never stand for anything awful happening to any child. I'd even go so far as to say that if there was a baby and she delivered it, she would have made sure that it was going to be well taken care of from there. And that she considered whatever went on confidential and isn't willing to break that confidentiality even now."

Kate didn't know if Ry believed any of that himself, but he didn't argue it. Instead he said, "Well, the bottom line is that I've struck out when it comes to getting any kind of proof that Gram *did* have a baby with that old SOB and that he took it away from her the way she says he did. That means that the best I can do from here is go back to Tyson and put some pressure on him."

"He's gone."

"Where did he go and how do you know?"

"I did a massage for his housekeeper today. She said she was at the start of a four-day weekend because Hector went to Las Vegas. He won't be back until late Sunday night."

"Then I'll get him on Monday," Ry said, unruffled, his determination unmistakable. "I was going to have to spend the weekend in your sleepy hole-in-the-wall anyway."

Kate glanced at him. *"Sleepy hole-in-the-wall?"*

He smiled wryly again and shrugged. "Well, that's what Northbridge is, isn't it?"

"I suppose *hole-in-the-wall* applies since Northbridge is small, but it's not the nicest thing I've ever heard it called. As for sleepy? We always have *something* going on," she said, nodding in the direction of the Town Square they were approaching as she drove back into the heart of town. "Tonight, for instance, begins a series of Shakespeare plays that the summer-school drama class from the college is going to do for the next six Thursday evenings. It's free and there are hot dogs."

Ry took a turn at laughing at her. "Shakespeare in the park *and* hot dogs? Whoa! The big city has nothing on you. And we can't miss it—find a spot and pull over."

She wasn't sure if he was being facetious. But the

weather was warm, the Town Square was full of people, and being a part of that seemed preferable to dropping Ry off and going home to Internet dating sites and a catalog of strangers. So Kate said, "Really?"

"Absolutely. I'm not much for Shakespeare but a hot dog in the park on a nice summer's night? I can go for that."

Kate ignored the inner voice telling her not to do it and pulled into the first spot across South Street from the Town Square.

"I'll even treat—to compensate you for not getting what you wanted out of Fiona," she offered as if that was the reason she was doing this.

Rather than because she just plain wasn't ready to part ways with him yet tonight.

Long before Kate had actually met Ry she'd had the impression that Northbridge had taken to him. By the end of that evening, she was convinced of it. And felt as if her night had been ruined because of it.

It was after ten o'clock before she and Ry left the Town Square. But as they got back in the car, Kate thought that she shouldn't have worried about spending more time with Ry tonight. It wasn't as if she really had.

Yes, they'd been together, but she didn't think there had been a single other person in the park who hadn't sought him out to talk or stopped him as they'd walked by or called or motioned for him to go to them. In short, she hadn't had a minute on her own with him.

Which should have been perfectly all right.

But somehow it hadn't been.

"Apparently Northbridge likes you more than you like Northbridge," Kate commented as she pulled out of her parking spot and headed for his grandmother's house to drop him off.

Ry angled in his seat and stretched his arm along the back of hers. "Did I say I didn't like Northbridge?"

"Sleepy hole-in-the-wall," she reminded him of his earlier words.

"That didn't mean I don't like Northbridge. It just means that I think small doses of it are going to be enough for me."

"Because it isn't what you consider exciting."

"As far as I can tell, people around here are *excited* over just having a new face in the mix. That shouts that this place is a snooze, doesn't it?"

"You're more than just a new face—we see new faces here fairly often and it isn't enough to excite anyone. But you...you swooped in here flying your own plane. Ever since Wyatt's wedding, I've been hearing about how you went on safari in Africa, and how you've been skydiving and deep-sea diving. How you've skied the Alps and climbed Kilimanjaro. Your sister and brother talk about all your escapades. And so do you, for that matter—last night with Celeste, there was your time in Greece to go with the ouzo, and tonight you said you threw out the first ball at a Rockies game in Denver. It all makes you more than just a *new face.*"

"Okay, so yeah, maybe a few things have come up. But just in the normal course of conversation. I wouldn't have said anything about Greece last night except that there *was* ouzo. And tonight the Rockies story came up when those guys were talking about baseball. The Rockies *are* a professional baseball team, you know?"

"I know. And you made it clear that you only got to throw out the first ball last year because Home-Max

The Reader Service — Here's how it works:

If offer card is missing write to: The Reader Service. P.O. Box 1867. Buffalo NY 14240-1867 or visit www.ReaderService.com

NO POSTAGE
NECESSARY
IF MAILED
IN THE
UNITED STATES

BUSINESS REPLY MAIL

FIRST-CLASS MAIL   PERMIT NO. 717   BUFFALO, NY

POSTAGE WILL BE PAID BY ADDRESSEE

THE READER SERVICE
PO BOX 1867
BUFFALO NY 14240-9952

GET FREE BOOKS & FREE GIFTS WHEN YOU PLAY THE...

SLOT MACHINE GAME

Just scratch off the gold box with a coin.
Then check below to see the gifts you get!

YES! I have scratched off the gold box. Please send me the 2 free Silhouette Special Edition® books and 2 free gifts (gifts are worth about $10) for which I qualify. I understand I am under no obligation to purchase any books, as explained on the back of this card.

We want to make sure we offer you the best service suited to your needs. Please answer the following question:
About how many NEW paperback fiction books have you purchased in the past 3 months?

❏ 0-2   ❏ 3-6   ❏ 7 or more

E4KQ   E4K2   E4LE

235/335 SDL

FIRST NAME	LAST NAME

ADDRESS

APT	CITY

STATE/PROV.   ZIP/POSTAL CODE

Visit us online at
www.ReaderService.com

7	7	7	**Worth TWO FREE BOOKS plus 2 BONUS Mystery Gifts!**
🍒	🍒	🍒	**Worth TWO FREE BOOKS!**
🔔	🔔	🍒	**TRY AGAIN!**

DETACH AND MAIL CARD TODAY!

® and TM are trademarks owned and used by the trademark owner and/or its licensee. © 2009 HARLEQUIN ENTERPRISES LIMITED. Printed in Canada.

became an advertiser at the field, and because you're friends with a few of the players—I heard the story. The point is, *that* is why you are the first nonlocal ever to be asked to play in one of the Bruisers games, it wasn't because the other guys are bored."

The Bruisers were the men's sports team that played football, basketball or baseball according to the season. The games were informal, with the men randomly dividing themselves up into two teams to play against each other. But informal or not, the games had become a staple of entertainment in Northbridge, and Friday kicked off their first baseball game of the summer.

"What I'm saying," Kate reiterated in defense of her town, "is that Northbridge is not such a dull place that just the fact that you're a new face causes a commotion."

"Okay, but still…you can't tell me *Northbridge* is an action-packed adventure."

"You haven't given it a chance," she accused.

"Tell me what I'm missing," he challenged.

Kate answered that one facetiously. "Randy Markey skateboards and has a half-pipe out at his dad's farm—want me to see if I can set up a playdate?"

Ry laughed in spite of her tone. "You worked wonders on my shoulder, but I'm not sure I'll be skating a half-pipe anytime soon. Thanks for asking, though."

Kate knew she'd been unnecessarily cutting. It was just that she was feeling contrary because she'd had to share him to such an extent tonight, and he didn't even appreciate the fact that it had been because the town she loved was so enamored of him.

"I'm just saying that you seem to think we're comatose here and we aren't. There are always a lot of things going on and a lot of things even someone like you could find to entertain themselves with."

"What, for instance, could *someone like me* find to entertain themselves with?" he said in a goading tone that let her know he was enjoying her annoyance.

"*For instance,* there's horseback riding, and once a year part of the rodeo circuit comes through and people from here can sign up for events. There's camping and fishing and hunting. There's off-road everything—bicycles, motorcycles, three- and four-wheelers. There's waterskiing out at the lake. Snow skiing in winter is only a half hour's drive from here. There's hiking. And there are more festivals and carnivals and town events than I can name, plus whatever the college does—like the play tonight and concerts. There are parties and dances and celebrations. And weddings—there have been a lot of those lately—"

"And don't forget Randy Whozits's half-pipe," Ry put in with some facetiousness of his own.

She knew he was teasing her because she'd begun to sound like a tourist brochure listing the activities available in Northbridge.

"So do *you* do all that stuff?" he asked then.

"Well, not the athletic things," she answered honestly.

"But the point is that you really like it here, and you think even *someone like me* should, too," he said, obviously knowing what was bothering her.

They'd reached his grandmother's house and Kate pulled into the driveway, putting the car into parking gear but leaving the engine running.

She took a breath and exhaled, trying to let go of the weird sense that she had to make him like her hometown.

She had no idea why it had suddenly become so important to her in the first place.

"I love Northbridge," she said simply. "It may not be exciting to you, but it's exciting enough for me."

"And there *is* that baseball game tomorrow night," Ry said, angling even more in the passenger seat now that they were parked, and still clearly amused by her. "Is that something you go to watch even though you don't *do* athletic things?"

"Sometimes," she said, when the truth was that she wasn't much for watching sports either and *didn't* make it a habit to go to the Bruisers' games.

"Will tomorrow night be one of those *sometimes?*" Ry asked enticingly.

The minute he'd agreed to play she'd begun to have thoughts about going but she didn't want to say that. So instead she said, "I don't know."

"It would make it more exciting if you did."

The smile that went with that was so boyishly disarming that Kate couldn't help smiling, too. Still, she said, "I doubt that anything would make it more exciting for you. Besides, I'd just be sitting in the bleachers with everyone else. It isn't as if I'd be in a skimpy cheerleader's outfit jumping around on the sidelines to stir things up."

"Now *that* I'd like to see!"

Kate rolled her eyes as if that didn't please her right to her toes.

"Come on," Ry cajoled in that way that always seemed to wear her down. "I guarantee that it would make it more exciting for me to have you there. And then afterward you can take me to Adz—the invitation to play came with the invitation to go there later."

"*I* can take *you?*"

"To show me more of what you think is so great about this place."

Of course all the reasons not to do that came instantly to mind. Again. Which they should have, because they were valid.

Yet once more those reasons didn't wipe away what she *wanted* to do.

And that was when it occurred to her that maybe she was taking the wrong course in trying to resist Ry's appeal. Maybe a better course would be to spend all the time she could with him. Maybe if she did that, it would bring home to her the multiple ways he didn't fit into her vision of the future, and then what she'd *want* would be distance from him so she really could get on with her plans.

Even if she did temporarily postpone her husband-hunting—for maybe just the weekend—that catalog of potential mates and the dating sites would still be there when she was finished, wouldn't they? And with no thoughts of Ry left to tempt her, she would be able to devote herself to them the way she needed—and wanted and intended—to. Without any distractions.

Okay, so maybe it was a little bit of a rationalization. But still, it made a certain amount of sense, too—especially since last night, before bed, she'd opened the catalog of men and rejected the first few because they hadn't been able to hold a candle to Ry Grayson. So getting her attraction to Ry Grayson out of the way first could only help.

She didn't think she should cave too easily to his request to go to the baseball game, though, so she said, "Maybe I will—it'll depend on what kind of day I have tomorrow."

"They must usually go pretty well or you wouldn't like it here so much."

"Oh, very slick," she said at his turning the tables on her.

He merely smiled, though. And he didn't push for a commitment for the next night—which set her slightly off balance again, the way his not kissing her the night before had.

And there she was, thinking about *that* again!

Maybe she should just stick to the dating services and the catalog after all.

Then, in a voice that had gone deeper and softer, and with a more tender smile that somehow drew her to look straight at him, into his eyes, Ry said, "You know what I think the best—and most exciting—thing about Northbridge is?"

Kate shook her head.

"You."

She had no idea what to say to that. And couldn't think of a single thing except how much she liked hearing it.

His arm was still resting on the top of her seat back, a fraction of an inch from her neck. She'd never been *un*aware of it, but she became instantly more aware of it than she had been before.

Plus, she didn't know exactly when he'd moved nearer, but he had. Near enough for her to be able to see every sharp angle and plane of his handsome face even in the dimness of her car interior. Near enough for her to smell his cologne and realize all over again how much she liked it.

Why *hadn't* he kissed her last night?

Then he said something she didn't understand at all. He said, "I never have been any good at staying in the safety zone," and with that, his hand cupped the back of her head to pull her toward him at the same time he leaned forward to meet her mouth with his.

It wasn't a no-holds-barred kiss. It wasn't a kiss charged with passion or heat. But it *was* a real kiss—not the there-and-gone kiss of the night before last. It was a kiss that lingered long enough for Kate to feel Ry's lips on hers, for her to feel the warmth of his breath against her cheek, for her to kiss him back.

But only a little and then he ended it.

His hand stayed a moment longer in her hair, massaging her head and making her think that he was considering a second kiss.

And while it was a struggle not to say *yes, please,* she succeeded, merely raising her chin to him slightly.

He didn't kiss her again, though. Instead he took his hand away and got out of the car.

But he didn't just close the door and leave, either. He bent back in to say, "Don't disappoint me tomorrow night."

"We'll see," she managed to say but it came out an unintentionally coy whisper.

That just made him grin as if he knew exactly what was going to happen the next night.

He finally did shut her door, though, and Kate sat for another moment, watching him go up to his grandmother's house.

She was still thinking about that kiss.

It hadn't been better than any kiss she'd ever had before—the way she'd thought another kiss from him might be.

But it had been a kiss good enough to leave her lips still sweet and warm and tingly.

A kiss good enough to make her want him to take another stab at it.

Go home before this gets any worse! she ordered herself when she began to imagine following him up onto that porch.

She took another deep breath and sighed it out audibly.

Then, with her engine still running—in more ways than one—she put her car into gear and backed out of the driveway.

Hoping as she did that she wasn't making a mistake by thinking that more time with Ry would be a turnoff.

Hoping that it didn't end up being an even bigger turn-on.

Chapter Eight

"**I**'m telling you, it's never happened before. Has it, Kate?"

Kate was at the Bruisers' baseball game on Friday night. She was sitting with Ry's brother Wyatt and his new wife, Neily—the former Neily Pratt, whom Kate had known all her life because they were both Northbridge natives.

It was Neily who was asking Kate to confirm that a non-Northbridge resident had never been allowed to even play in one of the games, let alone pitch the way Ry was doing at that moment.

"Neily is right," Kate answered.

"How did my fair-haired brother manage it then?"

Wyatt's question was for Kate, so she explained. "A bunch of the guys got all wound up last night when they heard that Ry had thrown a ball at a professional baseball game. It didn't seem to matter that he got to do it because he knows some of the Colorado Rockies' players and because Home-Max bought advertisement at the field. It still impressed them so much that—"

"Wait—" Wyatt said, "you think Ry got to throw the ball out at the Rockies game because Home-Max is advertising at Coors Field?"

"That's what Ry said," Kate informed him.

"That's not the reason why. I mean, yes, he is friends with some of the players, in fact he was on the college team and was scouted right along with them. But he got to throw out the first ball last season because he sponsors a sort of informal sports league for underprivileged kids and last year he raised the money and made all the arrangements to take 300 of them to that game—the season opener in Denver."

"Honestly?" Neily said, sounding as impressed as Kate felt.

"Yeah," Wyatt said, going on to brag about his brother by adding, "Ry has a hand in basketball, football and soccer leagues in the same vein—all for underprivileged kids. And now he's started a college scholarship program for them."

"I didn't know he liked children that much," Neily said. "Or got involved in charity kind of things for them. He must really want to be a dad."

"Oh, I don't know about that," Wyatt laughed as if he couldn't imagine his brother having children of his own. "I think it's more that Ry likes playing as much as any kid I've ever seen and just wants to pass it on."

"Still, I didn't know my new brother-in-law had a philanthropic side," Neily marveled, again voicing something Kate was thinking, too.

"There's more to Ry than you might think," Wyatt said proudly as his brother struck out his first batter. "All that surplus energy has to go somewhere. He also makes sure that Home-Max carries organics and environmentally friendly fertilizers, pest-control methods, cleaning solutions, paint—you name it, if there's something natural to offer alongside the traditional stuff, we're selling it. And because of him, every board foot of our lumber comes from companies that have what they call *best management practices*—that means that all logging is done within environmental guidelines to prevent destruction of the forests."

"I didn't know he was so into that, either," Neily mused.

Again Wyatt laughed. "Oh, yeah. Maybe he has a particular stake in protecting the earth because he kind of sees the whole thing as his playground."

The patch of it that he was standing on at that moment genuinely *was* playground—it was the baseball field that served the combined elementary, middle and high school. And from where Kate sat in the bleachers, she couldn't help appreciating the sight of the well-built, athletically gifted Ry, who was obviously in his element playing the game that they all went back to watching silently then.

But as they did, Kate was still thinking about what she'd just learned about Ry.

He cared about the environment and put effort into bringing a little joy into the lives of underprivileged kids?

Those were not the kind of things she wanted to find out about him during this hiatus from her husband hunt. Those were things she admired, things that impressed her.

Those were things that might have made her rethink her new plan to spend more time with him to discover his flaws. Finding *more* things she liked about him was definitely counterproductive to that.

But there he was, out on the baseball field, and she was feasting on the sight of him in scraggy old torn jeans and the white baseball shirt the team had loaned him.

And oh, boy, was she feasting.

If Ry had been the toast of the Town Square on Thursday night, it was nothing compared to the post-baseball-game celebration at Adz on Friday evening. He was being given credit for winning the game for his side—both with his pitching and with the two home runs he'd hit.

But after drinking the beer the team bought him as a reward, and giving an hour to reliving the highlights of every play, he leaned in close to Kate's ear and said, "I think we can duck out now."

That came as a surprise to Kate. She'd assumed they would stay at Adz with everyone else. Not that it was an unpleasant surprise since she wasn't any happier to share him with the crowd tonight than she had been last night.

Unless he intended to take her outside, say good-night and this was going to be the end of the evening.

Still, there wasn't much she could say except, "Okay, sure," before they began their exit from the packed bar and restaurant that was Northbridge's biggest hangout.

It took about twenty minutes for them to make it through the front door and onto the sidewalk where a few more post-gamers were getting some air.

Continuing accolades for Ry's skills delayed them a bit longer before he finally inched Kate away from those people, too.

Then, once they were out of earshot of everyone, he said, "So how about you show me your place?"

She was relieved that he wasn't merely going to say

good-night to her, but slightly taken aback. That suggestion had come out of the blue.

"My place?" she said, knowing she sounded dumbfounded because he grinned the way he did whenever the mischief-maker in him thought he'd stirred something up.

"Yeah. We could grab a bottle of wine or a six-pack and—"

"It's after ten o'clock—the liquor store is closed."

"Of course it is," he said. "Well, still, I've been wondering where you live, so let's go anyway."

"To my place…" she repeated suspiciously.

That just made his grin stretch. "No ulterior motives," he assured. "It's just that when I was searching the stands for a sign of you tonight, I thought that if you hadn't shown up, I don't even know where you live to drop by later."

"When were you searching the stands for a sign of me?" she said dubiously.

"When I was in the outfield—that's why I missed that ball that came my way—the one flub everyone keeps forgiving me for. I was looking for you, to see if you came."

Oh, so he hadn't been completely oblivious to her. She hadn't noticed that.

She didn't say it, though. She just went back to what he'd said before. "*Would* you have dropped by later if I hadn't come tonight?"

"To give you a hard time about not coming? Yes."

"I believe the *hard time* part."

"So what do you say? Show me where you live?"

She pointed a block up from where they were and toward the sky. "There," she said.

"You live in heaven? That explains so much," he teased.

"I rent the apartment above the hair salon."

Ry glanced at the building she'd indicated, then down at the rest of the street. "Most of what we've done this week has been somewhere along here and you've had your car every time."

"Yes, I have," she agreed.

"When you could have walked because none of it is more than a few blocks."

"Yes, but when I'm being the city clerk I can have papers to deliver to the mayor out at his farm, and when I'm being the massage therapist, I have elderly people who can't get to me, who I have to get to no matter how far out of town they are—*with* my massage table. I still need my car," she concluded.

"And tonight?"

"I walked."

"So we could just walk over to your place now," he said, getting back to the subject that had gotten them there in the first place.

"We could if I'd agreed to that," Kate said.

Ry smiled again—the smile she couldn't resist. "I'd still like to see it. I promise not to do anything that would raise the Reverend's eyebrows—does that help?"

"The Reverend would raise his eyebrows at you getting anywhere past my front door."

Ry leaned in to whisper, "I won't tell him if you don't."

Kate shook her head at him, knowing she was going to concede but stalling just to give *him* a hard time.

Then she said, "I don't have any beer or wine but I do have a pitcher of lemonade in the fridge."

"Good enough!" Ry decreed. Then he placed a palm against the small of her back to urge her toward her apartment.

Kate hoped she wouldn't regret this, but headed for home anyway.

"So where's the skimpy cheerleader's outfit?" Ry joked as they began to walk.

Once underway, he took his hand away from her back and she tried not to miss it. "If you'll recall, that's what I said I *wouldn't* do," she pointed out.

"You said you might not come, either. But here you are."

"Only *not* in a skimpy cheerleader outfit."

"It must be at the cleaners. But this is nice, too," he added, waving an index finger up and down her outfit of jeans—her tightest—and a scoop-necked tan T-shirt she wore over a white tank top that were both so formfitting they left nothing to the imagination.

"Gee, thanks," she responded to his teasing compliment.

She didn't tell him she liked the jeans he'd changed into after his post-game shower, or that she'd noticed that he was once again wearing an extremely expensive-looking blue-and-gray striped shirt that she thought might have been custom tailored for him. Instead, she said, "I thought your brother and Neily would come to Adz tonight, but they didn't."

"They're still newlyweds. I think they had better things to do. Plus they're driving back to Missoula early tomorrow morning so they didn't want this to be a late night."

"Wyatt drove all the way here from Missoula to pick up Neily?"

"Yep. She's taking a few days off from being North-bridge's social worker to help Wyatt pack so he can per-manently move here. He drove in while she worked today, they got to see each other tonight and they'll drive back together tomorrow. They don't like being apart and want every minute they can get together."

"They do seem happy," Kate said, thinking about their handholding in the bleachers and the closeness they seemed to share. About the wave of envy she'd felt....

"I think they *are* happy," Ry added. "Wyatt also wanted to talk to me about the lawsuit—"

"Against Hector?" Kate asked as they rounded the side of the beauty shop.

"Yeah. A while ago we notified Tyson of our intent to sue for restitution on the land he nearly stole from Gram. If he'd been more cooperative about divulging what went on between them personally, we might have reconsidered. But as it is, we're going through with it."

They'd reached the alley and Kate led the way to the whitewashed wooden staircase that ran along the back of the building to the second story.

"Northbridge really knows how to do an alley up right," Ry observed. "Celeste's and now this one—they might technically be alleys but they don't look like any alley I've ever seen."

Probably because they both had a brick-paved street that made them look cobbled, the rears of the buildings had all been painted white, the windows were all shuttered, the trash receptacles were enclosed and there were carriage lights every few yards to make them as bright as Main Street was.

"The town spruced them up a few years ago in a town-improvement effort," Kate said as they climbed the steps to her door.

Her apartment was a large studio that she kept spotlessly clean so she wasn't worried about what he'd find when she let him in. But because it *was* a studio apartment, the bedroom, living room and kitchen were all combined in the same space. And while the portion that was her bedroom was somewhat set off from the rest and raised a step higher, her bed was still right there in the open. She always worried that that might make it seem like an invitation even when she wasn't sending one.

So after Ry had looked around and commented on the place, she said, "It's been closed up, though, and it's stuffy in here. Why don't we take our lemonades and sit outside on the steps?"

Ry agreed easily enough and that was what they did, ending up side by side on the landing, both of them angled to rest their backs—Kate against the building, Ry against the railing.

Which also let Kate look at him in the golden glow of those carriage lights.

Liking that more than she wanted to, she set her lemonade on the landing between them and said, "You didn't tell me—or anyone else—the whole story behind throwing out that first ball at the Rockies game. It was really because of what you did to bring 300 underprivileged kids there to see the game."

Ry shrugged as if it was no big deal.

"Wyatt also told me you're responsible for getting Home-Max to do what they can for the environment."

Ry smiled and said as if he were confiding state secrets, "I recycle, too." Then he changed the subject. "It must have been a slow game if that's what you guys were talking about up in the bleachers."

Kate wasn't going to let him off the topic that easily. What little Wyatt had said had made her curious and she wanted to know more about this aspect of Ry.

Actually, she was hoping to find something—anything—about him that *wasn't* admirable and impressive—

So she said, "How did you get involved with sports for underprivileged kids?"

"Accidentally," he answered, conceding to her persistence. "And with basketball first, not with baseball—"

"But Wyatt said you were scouted to play professional baseball."

"Sounds like Wyatt did a lot of talking," he muttered. "Yes, I was scouted to play in the minors, but that's not where the kid thing started. That started when I put up a basketball hoop in the back of our main store. The hoop was meant for me and some of the other guys to play during breaks."

"Ah," Kate said because that was along the lines of what she expected—that it would have more to do with his own interests than those of the kids.

Ry didn't take note of it, though. He merely went on answering her question. "The store was near a public housing development and some neighborhood kids from there started coming around to use it—the younger, smaller kids who couldn't compete with the older, bigger kids who monopolized the hoops at the housing project. Kids who, for whatever reason, couldn't be involved in the Little League or peewee sports that the recreation centers offered. The guys and I would shoot with them sometimes or just watch them play. I got a kick out of them. I had a good time with them. I got to know them and saw that some of them had real potential. I wanted to help them out where I could."

"So you started a basketball team?"

"I started basically the same thing the Bruisers are—when there were enough kids, I divided them up into two teams to play against each other. Then more kids came around and there were three teams. Then four. It went from there."

"And the baseball?"

"Some of the kids weren't interested in basketball or were never tall enough to have fun playing, and I liked baseball, so I suggested that one summer. It grew the same way the basketball teams did. Football and soccer just seemed to follow somehow. After a while I also started to see the need the kids had for shoes and clothes and equipment. Wyatt and Marti wanted Home-Max to help, so we found a way for that, but I also did some fund-raising and some bartering, and to tell you the truth, it's all just snowballed. But like I said, it's great and I have a good time with it."

As much as Kate had been looking for this to be more about Ry than about the kids, that isn't what she ended up seeing. She thought that his pleasure in it was honestly secondary to what he provided for the kids. And there was nothing in that that she could find fault with to make her not like him.

So she gave up trying for the moment, and merely went on to satisfy her own curiosity.

"Wyatt said you're doing a college scholarship program now, too?"

"Yeah. My teams are for young kids—once they can play sports in middle school and high school they'd rather do that. But some of my guys would come back and put in their two cents' worth coaching and advising the newbies even after they'd moved on themselves. I had to make a rule early on that anybody who dropped out of school couldn't hang around the little kids. I know it didn't do anything to make any of them actually *stay* in school—these kids are up against too much for me to have that kind of influence—I just didn't like the message it sent to have them there. But when I saw the ones who did fight through and were getting close to graduating, but couldn't afford college and didn't have a way to get any other kind of scholarship, I wanted to help them out, too—"

"With a scholarship program of your own."

"I was raising money anyway. Why not raise some for that? You'd be surprised how big a check you can get a guy to write in a bar after a round of golf or in a country-club locker room when the big winner of anything is feeling full of himself. It isn't a huge program at this point, but it's something."

Then he smiled one of those ornery smiles again and said, "Why, were you thinking of going back to school and looking for some help?"

She was looking for help, but it wasn't to go back to school.

Instead of answering his question she said, "And the playing professional baseball thing? I'd think you'd jump at something like that. Did the scouts not pick you?"

"Actually, they *did* pick me," he said as if she'd gotten something not quite right about that. "I had an offer to play on a minor-league team with some talk of moving up to the majors in a pretty short time. But I opted for other things."

"Traveling to far-flung places and climbing steep mountains?"

"Working at Home-Max."

Kate laughed initially because she thought he was joking. But then she realized that he wasn't.

"You gave up a potential career in a sport you love to work in your family's hardware business? When you probably could have gone into that later on anyway?" Kate said in disbelief.

"Yep," he answered simply.

That wasn't what she would have expected of him, either. "How come?"

He shrugged. "Maybe it's the triplet thing. Or pride or ego or something. Whenever Wyatt and Marti and I had worked, it had been for the hardware business and together. When I finished college early I didn't want to go to work without them—that's why I traveled while they took their last semester. But I also didn't like the thought of them going to work without me if I went off to play baseball. I *like* working with them. We're good together. And yeah, I could have just come into the business when the baseball thing was over, but I'd have been coming into what they'd built up. I'd have been riding on their coattails. I didn't like the way that made me feel. I had fun playing baseball, but it wasn't the be-all and end-all of my life. But Marti and Wyatt? They're family. The business was the family business. That stuff mattered more. I can have fun everywhere. But family…that isn't something you can just blow off."

"Great, you were willing to sacrifice a potentially flashy career for family," she muttered to herself before she realized the words were coming out. It was just that she was thinking that this plot she'd hatched was not working if she kept discovering more things she liked about him.

Unfortunately, he'd heard her utterance. "What about that ticks you off?" he said, obviously confused.

"Oh, it's just that everybody seems to think you're some kind of superstar, and I'm trying to see the real picture," she said, not knowing what else to say to explain herself and hoping that accomplished it inoffensively.

"You want the inadequacies, the flaws and foibles, the imperfections and defects," Ry said.

"Well, yes." But so far, there weren't enough to help calm the attraction that seemed to gain strength with every minute she was with him. And she certainly hadn't uncovered any tonight. "I just want the good balanced with the not good—we all have that and I think it's better not to be blind to it."

"Agreed. Want me to tell you about my failings?"

"Yes," she said even as she couldn't keep from smiling and knew he was only going to come up with things that weren't what she was looking for.

"I'm a ball-hog when I play hoops. I ski and drive faster than I should. I like a long, hot shower and will use up all the hot water. I can be a pest. I'm a bear getting up in the morning. I'll pile on the jalapeños to a plate of nachos and then whine like a baby about the heartburn it'll give me. Put a salad in front of me and it's gonna sit there until hell freezes over because I hate 'em. The same with broccoli, cauliflower or peas. I fall asleep ten minutes into almost any period-piece movie, but give me the goriest, grossest, bloodiest vampires or werewolves and I'll watch it 100 times." He finished his lemonade and set his glass down. "Now you."

"You're looking for my failings, flaws, imperfections and defects, too?" Kate challenged.

He merely smiled.

"Okay, I suppose that's only fair. I eat cookies in bed every night before I go to sleep—and I don't share. I hate getting up in the morning, too, and will hit the snooze button an irritating number of times before I do. If I'm not hungry enough for a meal *and* dessert, I'll only eat the dessert. I like my green chile so hot it makes my eyes water and my nose run, and I don't care if it's yucky to sit across the table from me watching it. And when it comes to movies, I like to sit close to the screen and I've dragged my sister and my cousins and my friends to see things that have given them nightmares so now I mostly have to go to thrillers by myself. Which I do, and I still take up three seats even if the theater is crowded because I don't like taking the chance that anyone is going to talk to me through the movie—something I've been known to be very cranky about."

"Hmm," he said when she'd finished.

"What?"

"I just didn't expect there to be a little bit of a thrill-seeker in there with that hot green chile and scary movie stuff."

"A thrill-seeker is the last thing I am," Kate insisted.

"I don't know…. Sounds to me like you enjoy a little rush now and then."

Kate just shook her head at that idea.

Ry came away from the railing where his back had been resting, flexed his shoulders as if they'd begun to ache sitting there that way, and said, "That trouble-getting-up-in-the-morning thing should probably send me home—I have to meet with Wyatt before he and Neily leave at seven to give him some Home-Max paperwork that I still have to go by the store and get together."

"I take one Saturday a month off and tomorrow is that Saturday so I get to sleep in," Kate gloated to hide the fact that she hated that he was leaving, that just the idea of it also sent her thoughts wandering toward kissing again as if there were no question that it would happen.

He *was* leaving, though, because he stood then.

Kate stood, too, prolonging things by walking with him down the steps.

At the bottom of them he paused, turning to face her. "How do you spend your Saturdays off around here?"

"Puttering, mostly. Tomorrow I have an eleven o'clock haircut and then I'll go see Fiona—we're having lunch. After that I have some errands to run."

"Wow, that's a full day," he said facetiously.

She was half hoping he'd offer something better to do. With him.

Well, more than half. She was hoping it a lot. Especially since she'd already given herself permission to see him this weekend. And this weekend only.

But he didn't offer anything better to do. Instead he said, "I'll be at the store all day—if you're walking by, stop in."

She nodded, knowing she wouldn't do that. It was one thing to spend time with him if *he* instigated it. It was something else for her to seek him out.

His gaze went to her hair then, followed by a hand that brushed it over her shoulder. "You aren't cutting too much of this off, are you?"

"I'm only having it trimmed."

"Good. My grandmother has always said that a woman's hair is her crowning glory—I can't say I've really seen it before, but now I know what she was talking about."

Once he had her hair behind her shoulder, he didn't take his hand away. Instead it came to rest on the back of her neck, his fingers massaging sensuously as he looked into her eyes, delving into them.

"You may not share your cookies, but there are damn sure no defects here," he said in a voice that was barely audible and made her think that he might wish there were, the same way she wished she could see any in that sculpted face she'd tipped her chin to look up at.

Then he dipped downward and pressed his mouth to hers, kissing her again, answering a craving she'd had since the minute he'd stopped the night before, all in a way that seemed so right it was as if they'd done it a million times.

Only tonight's kiss wasn't a first-date kind of kiss. His lips parted farther than they had the previous night, waiting patiently for hers to part, too, coaxing them to. And when they did—as surely they had to because Kate couldn't keep them from it—his tongue came to toy with hers.

Temptation—that's what his tongue offered. An alluring invitation for her lips to open a bit wider, for the freedom to test the very edges of her teeth with it, for her tongue to come and meet his, tip to tip.

His other arm went around her, bringing her nearer, and Kate's hands went to his chest to lie flat on the so-fine fabric of that shirt, to feel the hard wall of his chest just behind it.

His hand at her neck rose into her hair, cupping her head as his mouth opened even wider. His patience evaporated and his tongue began a sexy, insistent frolic with hers. A sexy, insistent frolic that Kate kept up with, meeting him, matching him, rivaling him every step of the way. And reveling in it all.

No, she shouldn't be doing it—she knew that. But it didn't matter. She wanted to be. She wanted to be doing so much more with him that even that kiss seemed like a compromise to keep her from doing so much more.

Then, just when she was thinking about doing so much more anyway, he began to end the kiss.

His tongue took one final, slower circle of hers and retreated. Still, he went on kissing her for another moment— a wide-open and wicked kiss even without the tongues, before he stopped, returned for another, simpler kiss as if he just had to, and then reared back slightly.

But just when Kate was sure that was it, he tilted his head and ducked in to kiss her under her left ear, behind her jawbone, in a spot she'd never known to be so sensitive.

Sensitive enough to send a little tremor from there all the way through her.

Then he stood up straight, kissed her lips once more in a warm, brief finish, before he said, "Thanks for the lemonade," let go of her completely, turned on his heels and left.

Kate had to grab for the stair railing to keep her balance until the starch came back into her legs, all the while watching him go in a haze left behind by that kiss.

That kiss—and the one on her neck that had topped it off—this time really was better than any she'd ever had before.

Chapter Nine

"I think I better ask—when I get you back to that apartment, will there be police waiting?"

From the passenger's seat, Kate looked over at Ry where he sat behind the wheel of his sister's SUV. She had no idea what he was talking about. "Police?"

"I'm just wondering if by now they've found the *real* Kate Perry there, bound and gagged, while you impersonate her. I mean, surely the *real* Kate Perry would never have spent the last few hours doing what you have."

"Very funny," Kate said.

It was late on Saturday night and they'd just left Ry's private plane.

"I'm serious," he insisted. "I lured you out tonight figuring there was less than half a chance that I'd actually get you on my plane, and, yeah, it took some persuasion, but unless I'm reading it wrong, you *liked* flying. Now here we are, going back to your place for you to have sushi for the first time—the second thing tonight that I'm having trouble believing I got you to agree to."

He'd called late this afternoon and said there was something he wanted to show her. He'd said he'd pick her up in an hour.

Kate had made a mad dash to shower, do her hair, makeup and iron the wrinkles out of one of the new outfits she'd bought shopping that afternoon—a pair of navy blue capri pants that made her rear end look fabulous, and a pale blue, low-cut, V-necked T-shirt that she was wearing over a breast-shaping camisole that gave her a whole world of lift.

She'd barely been ready to go when Ry had arrived driving the vehicle his sister had left behind. When he'd taken Kate to his plane, she'd thought the plane was what he'd wanted to show her.

Instead—after some cajoling—he'd whisked her away in it, flying low over all of Northbridge so she could have the bird's-eye view of her hometown and the farms and ranches on its outskirts. Then he'd flown them to Bozeman where they'd stopped only long enough to have a cooler full of sushi delivered to the airport before they'd turned around and flown back to Northbridge.

Kate's only answer to his comment that he couldn't believe she'd agreed to it all was, "It's the weekend—everyone lets their hair down on the weekend." Particularly a weekend she'd granted herself ahead of time.

"Your hair isn't down—it's back in that curly-messy thing you did at the wedding," he noted.

"Letting my hair down was a figure of speech. Weekends are *for* relaxing and doing something fun."

"But you let me take you up in my plane," he persisted as he started the SUV and pulled away from the aircraft. "And not only weren't you the white-knuckled passenger I thought you'd be, you even did a little of the piloting."

"I had a steady hand, too, didn't I?" she said, not camouflaging her pride in herself.

Ry glanced at her out of the corner of his eye as he waited for a truck to pass before he eased onto the highway from the dirt road that ran through the field where he'd landed the plane. "Tell me now—the real Kate Perry is bound and gagged somewhere and you are her image from the other side of the mirror, aren't you?"

"I did refuse to eat any raw fish, if that makes me seem more like myself," she reminded him primly, referring to the sushi.

"I'm not sure that's enough to sell me on who you are."

"It's the best I can do," Kate said, enjoying herself still. Then, to explain her sudden letting loose, she said, "I've never flown before—"

"I still can't believe that," he said.

"I told you—I've only been outside of Northbridge on road trips. But I've always wanted to try flying. Being the pilot didn't look hard, so I thought I might as well try that, too. And if you were going all that way for takeout, I just figured I should give sushi a chance, especially since everybody I know is talking about it lately. But I'm not eating raw fish," she concluded forcefully.

"Your rolls are either vegetarian or have smoked salmon or shrimp tempura in them. But if you change your mind and decide to go whole hog outside-the-box tonight, I'd be willing to share."

Kate merely wrinkled her nose at him.

"Now *that* looks more like the real Kate," he goaded, turning onto Main Street. "And I don't see any cop cars or the rescue squad," he added as he drove nearer to her apartment. "But I still don't know...."

"Keep it up and I'll send you home to eat your raw fish alone," she threatened with no intention of doing any such thing.

Ry parked at the curb in front of the beauty shop. Kate didn't wait for him to come around and open her door, she got out herself while he opened the back door to retrieve a small Styrofoam cooler he'd brought with him to keep the sushi cold.

"Talk about things you can't believe—" Kate said as she led him around to the alley. "I can't believe you flew a plane for take-out food."

"I wanted sushi and there aren't a lot of places in Montana that serve it—the restaurant in Bozeman is the closest but hardly a quick drive," he said as if that alone made perfect sense of it.

"We could have just gone there for dinner," Kate pointed out. "Are you sure you aren't going to die eating raw fish that's just made this trip?"

He held up the cooler. "That's why I brought this, to keep it cool," he said. "If we'd just gone there to eat instead of using their extended take-out hours after they closed, you wouldn't have gotten the air tour of North-bridge on this beautiful summer night. That would have been a shame."

"I wouldn't have wanted to miss it," she acknowledged as they went up the stairs to her apartment, appreciating that he'd factored what she might like into the equation.

Anticipating that they might end up there again tonight,

she'd left the windows open and since it was still early summer, that had been enough to make the temperature perfect inside.

Kate turned on the lights and went to the kitchen for plates, silverware, napkins and glasses for the sake she'd also agreed to try.

"Let's eat sitting on the floor at the coffee table," Ry suggested as she did. "You'll feel like you're in Japan."

"I eat at the coffee table all the time and I never feel that way," she informed him without refusing.

She watched him from the kitchen as she gathered things, wondering how anyone could dress as simply as he was tonight—in jeans and a plain gray henley T-shirt with the sleeves pushed up—and still look so awe-inspiring.

He managed, though, and because Kate was thinking about that, she was late in realizing that she should have insisted they eat at her two-person kitchen table instead of at the coffee table.

Because only when Ry saw what was on the coffee table did Kate remember the catalog from Partner-Finders.

She'd found a message on her voice mail this afternoon after running her errands. It had been from the Billings matchmaking firm. A male client had requested an intro-duction to her. Kate had taken out the catalog and plopped down on the sofa to look him up.

In the course of that, Ry had called. She'd set the catalog on the coffee table and instantly forgotten all about it and the other man, putting her attention and energy into getting ready to go out with Ry.

So the catalog was still on the coffee table.

She'd remembered to cool the apartment off with Ry in mind. But she hadn't had a second thought about the catalog that potentially had her future husband in it—not a good sign, she told herself.

But regardless, of course Ry saw the catalog.

"What's this?" he asked, setting the cooler beside it and picking up what was essentially a three-ring binder with a cover that looked like an entertainment magazine called Find Your Perfect Mate.

Kate considered lying and saying that the catalog belonged to a friend who had left it behind.

But she didn't like lying. And lying about this made it seem as if she were ashamed of it, and she wasn't. Plus there was no reason to lie. She wasn't *dating* Ry. They weren't involved. They were just basically hanging out a little. It might even be a good thing to let him know she was looking for someone else so he had a clear understanding that she wasn't interested in him. Well, at least not beyond the time it took for her to get being interested in him out of her system.

So she said, "I joined a dating service called Partner-Finders. Those are the pictures and backgrounds of the men who also belong."

Ry looked at her as if he wasn't sure he'd heard her correctly. "Come on…you're kidding, right? *You* need a dating service? If someone like you, who looks like you do, can't get a date in this town, then I *know* there's something wrong with this town."

"It doesn't have anything to do with Northbridge or with anything being wrong with me. I joined because I thought it was an efficient way to get what I want," she said, not offering the information that she'd also subscribed to two Internet services, too. It was one thing to be honest, another thing to seem desperate.

She went into the living room and set the stack of dinnerware near the cooler. Then she picked up the catalog to put it on the corner table that formed the sofa and the easy chair into an L-shape, hoping that would be enough to end their discussion of this.

It wasn't.

"You joined a dating service for *efficiency?*" Ry said, still sounding confused as he began to take containers out of the cooler. "You want to *date* efficiently?"

"I'm through with dating *in*efficiently," she said.

"Couldn't dating just be fun?"

Of course that's the only way he would see it.

"Yes, dating could just be fun, but for me it needs to serve a purpose, too."

With all the food out and the places set, they sat on the floor to eat—Ry with chopsticks and Kate with a fork. For a moment Ry was more interested in advising her on how to best eat the sushi, encouraging her to add a dab of wasabi to each section of the roll, and then to dip it in soy sauce.

But just when she thought the dating conversation might have been left behind for talk of how, yes, she did like the sushi but, no, she still wouldn't try the raw fish variations, Ry returned to the topic.

"Sure, I suppose dating is *intended* to serve the purpose of *finding a partner,* but I've never seen it as a project— the way you make it sound. And why is it that way for you—are you in some kind of hurry?"

"As a matter of fact, I am." She decided that if she was going to be honest, she might as well be completely honest. "I want to get married and start my family, and I'm not willing to waste any more time."

He smiled as if something about that struck him as

funny. "The clock isn't just ticking, a bomb could go off at any minute?" he joked.

"Half a bomb has already gone off," she muttered as she took another tempura roll.

"Uh-oh…that sounds bad. What does it mean?"

Honesty was one thing, getting personal enough to explain that to him was something else. She wasn't sure she wanted to go that far. So she said, "Let's just say that after my history with men and *dating,* I've decided to take a different approach so that I can find someone who I know for sure wants the same things I want."

"Marriage and family—right *now,*" Ry said. "I take it that means you haven't dated anyone who was in that big of a hurry?"

"It isn't as if I've rushed anyone. The opposite, in fact. That's the problem—I've been blindly patient and it's cost me and I'm not going to let it happen again."

"Blindly patient," he repeated after eating another of his own rolls with considerably more wasabi on it than Kate could handle herself. "What exactly does that mean— blindly patient?"

"It means that I've let myself be miserably strung along—*three times*—and I'm not going to let it happen again. I can't afford to and I don't want to."

"How were you strung along?"

"First by my high-school sweetheart—Tommy Dobbs—"

"Wasn't the guy you ran away to marry—The Thug— named something else?"

"Roland—I ran away to marry him the summer *before* my senior year. But I don't count Roland among the three because that was different—it wasn't a formal engagement that anybody backed out of, it was just a teenage rebellion drama. There wasn't any *real* expectation that we would end up married."

"Okay. So after that you moved on to Tommy Dobbs, your *next* high-school sweetheart. You wanted to marry him and have kids with him in high school?"

"I didn't want to actually get married and have kids during my senior year of high school, no. But it was what I knew I wanted even then. It's how I've seen my life, all I've ever wanted—"

"Which is why you even chose your career based on it," Ry said, surprising her by remembering that and applying it here. "I guess it also shouldn't come as news—I'm betting that that's the way the girls in your family were raised, if the Reverend had any say in it."

"Yes, I'll admit that," she said. "But it's also what I *want*. A simple life, here in Northbridge, with someone as devoted to me as I would be to him. I respect that other women want high-powered careers and job success—my sister Meg has advanced degrees and a career she's thrived on, and I'm proud of her for that. But I have forever seen myself with a family, raising a bunch of kids, ending up half of one of those old white-haired couples sitting hand-in-hand on a bench in the Town Square looking out over those kids and their kids and maybe even the great-grandkids. *That's* what I have just always known instinctively is right for me. What will be the most fulfilling for me."

Both of Ry's eyebrows arched as if he wasn't quite sure what to say to that so Kate spared him and went on. "That's why I joined Partner-Finders—" And the other services she didn't want him to know about. "My plan is to only take under consideration—and use up any of my time with—men who are as focused as I am and who sincerely want what I want and are ready to settle down right now to have it."

"You really are in a hurry."

"I'm just not—"

"Going to be strung along again," he finished for her. "So tell me how you've been strung along—*three times*— *not* counting The Thug and beginning with Tommy Dobbs. Who I believe I met, didn't I?"

"You played baseball with him—he's one of the Bruisers."

"And he was your high-school sweetheart," Ry said to urge her to go on.

He also poured her a splash more sake and since she'd decided that she liked the liquor, she took a sip of the second glass before saying, "Tommy asked me to Homecoming our senior year. It was after my running away to be with Roland that summer and my first chance to socialize again when my grounding was finished. Anyway, Tommy's friends were taking my friends, and he figured it rounded out the group, so he asked me. Going in a group and not letting my family know I actually had a date was the only way I could get permission but Tommy and I really hit it off and we ended up being a couple from then on. We didn't even do the on-again, off-again thing that happens with kids—when we started, we stuck. So of course we planned to get married."

"Right out of high school?" Ry asked as if he thought that was a horrible idea.

"We got engaged at graduation. I would have married him a week later, but that wasn't what Tommy had in mind. He said nobody else was getting married—"

"And I imagine it was true."

"Actually, it wasn't. There were a few people who

actually did get married that summer. But for Tommy, *nobody* meant the group of friends who were really the center of the universe for him. *The Guys*—by the end, I wanted to scream every time he said that."

"Are the Bruisers The Guys?"

"The Guys are all on the team, but not everyone on the team is one of The Guys. The Guys are just Tommy's circle. His brothers, his closest friends. But that's all I ever heard from him—sure, he'd like to spend the day with me, but he was going hunting or fishing with The Guys. An evening alone? That sounded good, but he told The Guys he'd meet them at Adz. A movie? Maybe another night, he was shooting hoops or playing baseball with The Guys. And even when he would finally agree to a date night, he always just wanted to end up at Adz where we'd find The Guys." Kate sighed, unable to say *The Guys* even now without disgust.

"I get the picture—The Guys took priority. How long did you take that?"

"We were engaged for four and a half years—the longest engagement in town. It was a running joke." That still made her cringe to think about.

"What happened to call it off?"

"I finally put my foot down and said I wanted a firm date. Tommy wouldn't do it," Kate said quietly. "His older brother had gotten married during the time we were engaged, Shawn and his wife had even had a baby. But that was the problem—when Shawn got married, he spent less and less time with The Guys, doing The Guy things. And Tommy hated that. His friends were his life—that was what he said when I gave him the set-a-date ultimatum. He didn't want to end up married, with no time for The Guys, to do The Guy things, the way his brother had."

"So he opted for breaking up," Ry guessed.

"I imagine that we could have stayed engaged indefinitely," Kate said wryly. "But since that didn't seem like the best choice for me, I gave him his ring back. To this day he's doing exactly what he was then, with any of The Guys who can get away from the things they've moved on to. But moving on with his own life just doesn't seem to be what Tommy's inclined to do. He's still the same person he was in high school."

"Don't you think that if you had married him, you'd be at home alone with the kids while he did that same stuff anyway?"

"Yes," she acknowledged. "And I would probably still be waiting for Tommy to grow up—I saw at the end that that was the real problem and I'm not saying that I regret that we didn't get married, but it was—"

"Four and a half *years* of waiting," Ry finished for her, in tune with what she was thinking. "Then what? Did you move right on to string-along number two?"

"No. There was some dating in between. But nothing that clicked. Until Doug the dentist." Kate stood to clean up the dinner remnants and Ry did, too, following her into the kitchen as she said, "That was before we had a full-time dentist and Doug was the dentist who came into town from Billings twice a week. I cracked a tooth and—"

"Love blossomed?"

"Not instantly. But I liked him. And he was seventeen years older than I was—when he asked me out I thought he couldn't possibly be maturity-impaired at forty, and I accepted."

"Maturity-impaired?" Ry repeated with a laugh.

Kate merely shrugged. "That's what the men in my life have seemed to be. Not my brothers, or *all* the men I know, just the ones who I've been involved with. They're men who just aren't really adults."

As they finished in the kitchen and returned to the living room, Ry said, "But age didn't equal maturity with string-along number two?"

Kate knew she probably should have sat in the easy chair and left Ry alone on the couch. But she didn't. In fact, she didn't even sit at one end of the sofa, she sat in the middle, at an angle. And so did Ry, leaving them facing each other with his arm stretched along the top of the back cushion.

"What Doug really seemed to think," she continued then, "was that being with me somehow canceled those other seventeen years he'd lived and made him instantly my age instead of his. And now he had some things to prove. That was *his* thing—playing any competitive sport he could play and showing the world that he was the best, that he could beat anybody at anything, but particularly anyone younger than he was. And I was part of that—he was beating younger guys out of having me. Anyway, all of that was less a problem than our having kids—"

"He was too old?" Ry said with a kind smile, easing the tension by making a small joke.

"That was sort of what I thought," Kate agreed, laughing a little herself. "Not that he was too old to have kids, but that he was old enough that we shouldn't wait long after the wedding to start. Which was what I told him as the wedding got close." Kate sighed. "That was when he said that he thought nothing aged anyone as much as kids, that we were good together, why did we have to mess it up being parents?"

"Goodbye Doug the dentist?"

"It wasn't quite as simple as that. Other than the competitiveness and the age weirdness, Doug was a good person and I loved him. I wanted a family with him. There were a lot of heated discussions, but Doug couldn't be budged—marriage was one thing, he'd decided that kids were a no-go for him."

"So it was back to the dating pool?"

Kate nodded.

"Was that where you found string-along number three?" Ry asked as he poured them each more sake and handed Kate her glass.

She was getting light-headed but it helped her tell this without reliving the worst of the emotions that went with it. And she was going to need all the help she could get talking about number three.

"T.C. Cyr—Theodore Calvin Cyr," Kate said in a lower voice. "He was a friend of Noah's who came in to work on a big job Noah had remodeling the school."

"Another boy in man's clothing?"

"I didn't think so. T.C. was twenty-six, quiet and kind of stoic. He wasn't competitive or youth-obsessed or into all the sports that Doug had been into. He wasn't attached at the hip with any guy friends like Tommy. He *seemed* mature enough—maybe that's why it hit me as hard as it did to find out he wasn't. But then a lot of things hit me pretty hard with T.C."

Ry brushed the side of her face with the knuckle of his index finger, and said in a sympathetic voice, "This one was the tough one."

"None of them were easy. But yes, this one was particularly tough."

Kate hesitated. She'd avoided saying this earlier. But she'd come this far and, personal or not, this piece of the puzzle was too integral to leave out, so she conceded to telling him.

"I got pregnant."

Up went those eyebrows again, showing Ry's shock.

"It was an accident—birth-control malfunction," Kate explained. "We knew it had happened but I wasn't really worried that I might have gotten pregnant. We'd been dating over a year, I loved him and he said he loved me. We were talking seriously about getting married, so I thought that if I was pregnant it wouldn't be such a big deal—we'd have a quick, uncomplicated wedding and everything would be great."

Ry went on stroking her face. "But it wasn't."

"It definitely wasn't great," Kate said quietly. "I *had* gotten pregnant. But before I even knew it for sure, I started having a lot of pain. The pregnancy was ectopic—I don't know if you know what that means—"

"It means it was in the fallopian tube. And it isn't good."

"No, it isn't. I had to have emergency surgery to remove the pregnancy. And the tube."

"Ah…half a bomb," Ry said, repeating her earlier remark. "Just like that your fertility was reduced by fifty percent."

Kate was impressed that not only was he listening, he was seeing things through her perspective. "Just like that," she confirmed quietly.

"And T.C.?"

Kate shook her head. "Apparently he'd been panicking since the birth-control malfunction—although he'd hidden it from me. But in the hospital after my surgery he said he'd come to the conclusion that he wasn't ready to be *tied down,* that he couldn't handle the responsibility of a wife and kids. He said he felt as if he'd just dodged a bullet, as if he'd gotten lucky. That he couldn't be somebody's *father,* when, inside, he was just a kid himself."

Kate's voice cracked but she shook her head, refusing to let the painful memories get any more of a hold on her. "That one took me by surprise. With Tommy and Doug, there had been so many other things pointing to their maturity impairment. But with T.C...I couldn't believe he wasn't ready. But he was so *not* ready that he just wanted as far away from me and what I wanted as he could get. He was packed up and out of town by the time I was back on my feet."

Kate took another drink of the sake and set her glass on the coffee table, buying herself a moment to get things under control but knowing she'd better put an end to the drinking, too, because she was getting drunker than she liked to be.

Then she made an effort to sound more matter-of-fact again and said, "After that I decided I was going to take the bull by the horns myself. That that was it—no more wasting time with men who were not actively looking to settle down, to get married and have kids. And a dating service just seemed like the best way to do that because I've put it right up front that that's what I want, and unless the men have, too, I won't even consider them."

Ry smiled understandingly. "Is that it in the way of your qualifications? Wanting to get married? Can the guy be a troll or make his living as a hit man as long as he's marriage- and kid-minded?"

That helped lighten the tone, too, and made Kate smile back at him. "I haven't specifically excluded trolls or hit men, but I probably wouldn't be inclined to give them a date just because they want to get married and have kids, no. I'm fairly open, though. Except that I've also made it clear that I want to live in Northbridge, so any guy would have to be willing to relocate here."

"You know that's gonna narrow the field considerably," Ry warned.

"Not necessarily."

She could tell Ry disagreed with that but he didn't argue it. Instead he said, "So, can I harsh a buzz or what? I get you to let your hair down for the weekend and take you flying, get you sushi, then make you talk about this stuff."

"Yeah, what were you thinking with that?" she accused.

He nodded in the direction of the Partner-Finders catalog on the end table. "I was just trying to understand the dating-service thing." His smile turned into that mischievous grin of his. "Now I'm wondering if I better join."

Because of her? Was that what he meant?

Kate wasn't sure. But she didn't end up finding out because Ry's hand went from stroking her face to cupping the back of her head as he leaned forward to kiss her.

At first there was just comfort and consolation and maybe some apology for bringing up things that had been painful for her. But that didn't last long before Ry's lips parted, before Kate's parted, too, before kissing the way they'd kissed the previous night was what they were doing even if that hadn't been the original intention.

Tongues were playing and Kate's hands were against Ry's chest. Ry's other arm came around her, pulling her closer, and Kate went willingly.

Maybe it was the fact that everything was out in the open with him now, maybe getting it all out in the open had lifted some sort of weight off her shoulders; certainly there was the influence of the sake, but kissing him at that moment was just what she needed. It was just so, so nice. And it *was* the weekend. And she'd already opted to explore things with him in order to get past it so she could move on.

She wrapped her arms around him, laying her palms on his broad, honed back, closing a little more of the distance between them as the kissing deepened and there was less play and more intensity.

Oh, but the man could kiss! And his fingers were pulsing into her scalp in a sensuous massage. And his hand on her back was squeezing and kneading and making her think of other places where that would feel awfully good.

Her nipples were hard little pebbles straining within the built-in bra of her camisole. Straining for more than the chance to meet his chest. Putting in a bid for some of what his hand was doing to her back.

The sake had definitely loosened her up. But everything just felt too good for Kate to fight it.

His tongue was doing a slow, sexy dance with hers, and Kate was answering in kind, inviting more with the deep breath she took that brought her breasts into just a hint of contact with his chest.

But if Ry realized it had been an invitation, he didn't accept. He merely went on kissing her so intently, so thoroughly, that the yen for even more just got worse and worse.

Kate did some massaging of her own. Of his broad shoulders. Of his impressive biceps. Of his chest.

He smiled even as he was kissing her. She felt it. And she knew he knew what she wanted. But he was a devil and rather than giving it, his hand dipped from her back to her rear end—pausing to do some squeezing there instead—before he scooped her in closer still and ran that same hand along the back of her thigh to bring it over his legs.

Their mouths were open wide and their tongues were more assertive, bolder, as Ry's hand began an agonizingly slow ascension from her thigh, to her hip, to the side of her waist.

Kate wanted that hand on her breasts so bad she almost put it there herself. But she didn't. She just waited while the wanting grew and grew, until at last Ry finished the journey up and forward, finally finding her breast to cup in a warm, firm grip that molded perfectly around her.

Perfectly except for the layers of clothing between her flesh and his.

It felt good. Good enough for her to push into his palm as he reproduced that kneading, that massaging. But not as good as when he deserted her for a split second to find his way underneath both the T-shirt and the camisole and come back.

Kate moaned. It just felt too good not to as her nipple and every nerve stood on end to meet him and was rewarded with stroking and teasing and caressing and gentle tugs that all worked together to awaken everything inside of her, to make her want even more.

Did he want more, too? she wondered. And all on its own her thigh moved farther up his lap.

But before it got too far, Ry's hand left her breast to stop the rise of her leg and he went from kissing her mouth to nibbling the side of her neck as he said, "Only if you're sure the real Kate Perry won't have regrets tomorrow."

His hand was merely resting on her thigh. She still could have moved the rest of the way up.

And she wanted to. She wanted to press against him. She wanted his hand on her breast again. She wanted his mouth there, too. She wanted clothes to disappear and bodies to meet and…

She wanted it all.

But was she sure the sake didn't have something to do with that?

She was definitely feeling its effects so she couldn't be positive. And one thing she knew she didn't want was to wake up tomorrow and regret anything.

He was doing such lovely things at her neck, though….

Still, she moved her leg off his, sighed, and said, "I did have a lot of sake…."

He kissed his way down to her collarbone. He kissed his way along the edge of the V of her T-shirt. And if the T-shirt and camisole hadn't been there, it would have been mere inches more to kiss his way to her nipple.

But the T-shirt and camisole *were* still there and so he stopped kissing her altogether after planting one last one at the hint of cleavage.

"And here I liked that you were willing to drink tonight," he lamented.

Then he took a big breath, exhaled with resignation and got to his feet, pulling her with him.

"Tell me how to fill a lazy Sunday in Northbridge after my Scrabble game with Gram tomorrow afternoon so I don't just go to work for the seventh day in a row," he said as he took her with him to her door.

It was a bit more of a struggle for Kate to get her wits about her again and think of anything beyond him and her own needs.

But when she managed, she said, "I have church in the

morning and I see Fiona in the afternoon. And I usually do laundry on Sunday nights but I *could* make a picnic supper to have in the park."

He *had* treated her to a lot of meals this week, so she owed him, she rationalized. Plus in the Town Square, they would be out in public so nothing that shouldn't happen could happen. But she'd still be able to finish out this weekend with him.

"When shall I pick you up?" he said.

She told him. Then he just stood there at her door, looking down into her eyes, smiling a mystery-man smile.

And Kate wanted him to kiss her again so much she could hardly stand it.

But it was probably better that he just raised her hand from where he was holding it beside their thighs and kissed that alone before he said he would see her the next night.

Then he left and Kate closed the door behind him, standing there a moment longer, knowing she wasn't completely sober and that because of that she'd probably done the right thing in sending him home.

So why didn't it *feel* like the right thing?

Or at least like anything she was glad she'd done.

Instead she was just wishing he hadn't gone. That he was still there with her.

Holding her.

Kissing her.

Touching her everywhere.

He isn't The One, she reminded herself.

But at that moment she wasn't sure it mattered.

Chapter Ten

"So you can cook *and* play a mean game of volleyball."

Kate smiled at Ry marveling at her skills as they walked back to her apartment Sunday evening. They'd taken the picnic dinner she'd prepared—fried chicken, potato salad and biscuits—and spent the last few hours in the Town Square. As had been the case every other time they'd been in public, Ry was a popular visitor to Northbridge. Tonight he'd been in demand for volleyball games. And Kate had played, too.

"It's my grandmother's recipe for fried chicken—my mother's mother. And I grew up with two brothers so it wasn't all dollhouses and tea parties. I can hold my own—if I have to—at a lot of things."

"I'm beginning to see that," Ry said as if it intrigued him.

"I hit your bad shoulder pretty hard, though, when we collided. How does it feel?"

"Like it needs some attention."

Kate wasn't sure if that was true or if he was just using it as an excuse since there was some innuendo in his tone. But it wasn't as if she hated the thought of getting his polo shirt off in order to oblige him.

"I can check it out and see if we did any damage," she offered. "If not, I have a lotion with some pain-relieving stuff in it that will probably help."

"Ah...the advantages of being bashed by my masseuse," he said as they climbed the steps to her place.

She'd left the windows open again so the apartment was cool. The first thing Kate saw when they went in and she'd turned on the table lamp beside the sofa was the bunch of wildflowers Ry had brought her.

She nodded in their direction as she went to take the picnic basket to the kitchen. "Every time you start to tell me about picking those flowers today something interrupts and you never finish. Want to try again?"

"What I keep trying to get at is that I actually lured Gram out of the house to do it," he said, sitting in the center of the sofa and clearly making himself at home. "There's a whole patch that grows just down the hill behind the house—not where there was any chance of her meeting anyone—but still, I think it was a coup that I got her farther than the porch."

"I'd say that counts," Kate said.

She asked if he wanted anything to drink. When he declined she went to the bathroom for the lotion she'd mentioned on their way home.

When she rejoined him, Ry pointed a thumb at his shoulder and said, "Now?"

"Whenever you're ready," she responded as if it made

no difference to her. Then she bolstered herself for the baring of his chest.

She'd already seen it when she'd given him his initial massage so she knew how impressive it was. But now there were so many other things about him that had impressed her—and gotten to her—that she wasn't sure what this second glimpse of it was going to do to her.

Ry crossed his arms over his middle, grabbed the hem of the navy blue knit shirt and peeled it up and over his head.

"Your range of motion seems good," Kate observed, wishing her voice hadn't cracked slightly when she'd said that. But it had been only slight. Maybe he hadn't noticed.

"It's a little sore but I don't think you were as rough on it as the skateboard and the half-pipe."

Skateboard…think of him skateboarding like a kid, she advised herself as her eyes feasted on broad, straight shoulders, honed pectorals, biceps from heaven and his well-carved abs.

It didn't help. She might still be worried that there was more boy than man inside the body, but the body was all man.

Gorgeous, muscular man.

She silently cleared her throat before saying, "I want to feel the shoulder while I move your arm around."

"Be my guest." And of course he was smiling wickedly and there was a suggestive intonation in his voice.

Kate pretended to be all business. "Tell me if there's any pain," she instructed as she did what she'd told him she needed to do, letting one hand judge what was going on with his shoulder as she used her other hand to guide his arm through a series of tests. Trying as she did not to think about the heat of his skin or how smooth it was.

"Gram did some talking while we picked the flowers,"

he said, continuing with their conversation as she assessed his shoulder, convincing Kate that her touch had no effect on him. "She said Tyson brought her wildflowers."

"So they made her think of him?" Kate said, the best she could come up with under the circumstances.

"Seemed like it." Ry shook his head in disbelief. "She must have flashed on something good about him—for a minute she kind of drifted off, staring at the flowers and smiling."

Had his voice gotten a hint deeper by the end of that? Kate couldn't be sure.

"Pain?" she asked.

"Nothing you won't be able to take away with that lotion," he assured.

She could have told him to put the lotion on himself. But she reasoned that watching him do it wouldn't be much less of a turn-on, so she decided to just go ahead rather than make a big deal out of it.

She let go of him, squeezed out some of the lotion and warmed it between her hands. Then she did a mini-massage of his shoulder, fighting the inclination to expand her scope to include the rest of him.

"Oh...you're good," he said.

As a medical massage therapist, she reminded herself the way she'd reminded him so many times when he'd found out what she did for a living and teased her about it.

Kate tried to distract herself from the things that were coming awake in her by returning to the subject of his grandmother again. "But only for a minute?"

"Only for a minute?" Ry said as if he were lost in something of his own.

"You said that for a minute your grandmother drifted off and smiled when she saw the flowers."

"Oh. Right. Yeah, only for a minute. Then she bottomed out again and wanted to go inside. But at least while she was out there, she got some fresh air for a change."

The lotion was rubbed in by then but it took Kate a moment to make herself stop the massage. She knew she had to, though, so she put some effort into it and said, "Okay?"

"Sure," he answered as if he was none too happy to have it end, either.

But Kate took her hands away and sat on the sofa with him, angled in his direction as Ry put his shirt on.

Why Kate felt robbed when he did, she didn't want to analyze. Or show. So she said, "You're still set on seeing Hector again tomorrow?"

"That's the plan," Ry answered as he took a deep breath and sighed it out for no reason she could be sure of. "I'm going to tighten the screws and see if that'll get us anywhere."

"Maybe you should try a different approach—if Hector and your grandmother *did* have feelings for each other, maybe you could appeal to some remnant of those feelings in him."

She could tell by Ry's expression that he didn't think that would work. "Maybe. But on the other hand, potentially either Tyson used Gram's feelings for him to swindle her and take her baby away from her—in which case he's not likely to admit anything without some incentive. Or they had feelings for each other that ended on a really sour note—and in my experience, relationships that end on sour notes don't leave people too cooperative."

"Your experience." Now *that* was something interesting enough for Kate to sink her teeth into—and stop thinking about how he looked without a shirt. "I'll bet you've had enough experience to leave a symphony of sour notes behind to back that up," she said as if she were joking when she wasn't.

"I have not!" he said, taking issue as he raised a jean-clad leg to the couch so he could face her more fully and laid his arm across of the top of the back cushion, inches from her but not touching her. The way she wished he would.

"You've had very few experiences or you've left every woman in your life happy?" she asked for qualification.

"I've had a number of *experiences,* and I've left a few women *un*happy with me, but I'm careful about people's feelings and I've only caused one major war wound that I'm aware of—which is *not* a whole *symphony of sour notes.*"

"One major war wound, huh?" Kate said as if that were more than enough.

"Yes, but just one," he repeated.

"Let's hear about it," she demanded.

"Since you asked so nicely…" he said facetiously. "Her name was Paula. She was Wyatt's first wife's sister—an outdoorsy, super-athletic girl who had gone through college on a women's basketball scholarship, and coached high school girls' basketball in Missoula. She did just about everything I do in the way of sports and recreation, and since most of the women I date are particularly active—I usually meet them on the golf course or the tennis court or somewhere like that—Wyatt thought she'd be perfect for me. He hooked us up right after he and Mikayla got engaged."

"And *was* Paula perfect for you?" Kate asked, knowing it was insane that jealousy was itching at her.

He shrugged. "She could keep up with me—she would have been on that skateboard, in that half-pipe ahead of me last week, that's for sure. And she would never have let me live it down if she was better at it—there was some of that competitive thing you found in Doug the dentist in Paula, too. But that was okay, her energy and activity level meant that anytime of the day or night I had someone to—"

"Play with?" Kate said, unable to keep a bit of an edge out of her voice as that jealousy became a full-blown irritation.

"Yeah, *play with*," Ry repeated, rolling his eyes at her term. "Racquetball, tennis, golf, Ping-Pong, *volleyball*—" he added pointedly, "day or night, I had someone to *play* with."

"She *sounds* perfect for you. I'm surprised you didn't marry her."

"So was she. And everybody else, for that matter. We were together for almost two years—and yes, that was my longest relationship—when Paula said she thought it was time for us to tie the knot."

"Here it comes," Kate predicted. "But you don't see yourself ever settling down, getting married, having kids."

"That isn't it," he denied without a second thought. "I do see myself settling down, getting married and having kids someday—"

"When you grow up."

"Hey! I'm taking a lot of shots here," he chastised good-naturedly.

"Okay, I'm sorry," Kate said, knowing she *had* gone a little overboard. It was just that jealousy was eating at her even as she was anticipating him saying what she'd heard herself too many times, and she was trying to counteract it all by keeping in mind why she wasn't supposed to care whether or not he would ever settle down.

Then Ry said, "It's *because* I'm already *grown-up* that I could see the strengths *and* the weaknesses in my relationship with Paula. Yes, we had the sports thing in common and that made it look as if we were really compatible and connected. But what you and I are doing—" he waved an index finger back and forth between them "—just talking and being together without anything else going on? If Paula and I *weren't* doing something…physical…we were at a loss with each other. On anything but a surface level, there just wasn't anything going on for us. And *because* I'm already *grown-up,* I also recognized that my feelings for her weren't the kind to base a lifetime on. They'd been enough to base some good times on, yes— which is what we'd had. But *not* a marriage or a family."

There was something so reassuringly definite in that that it helped ease the jealousy.

"So she said 'let's get married' and you said no," Kate summarized.

"That's about it. And then there was far-reaching hell to pay."

"The breakup didn't go well?"

"Nooo, it didn't," Ry confirmed. "The intensity Paula poured into sports—and the physicality she put into things—translated into a golf club through the windshield of my car."

"That *is* intense," Kate agreed sympathetically.

"And it would have been bad enough to deal with, but to make matters worse, by then Wyatt and Mikayla were married so there were the family ties."

Kate could see that that had affected him more than the breakup. The frown lines between his eyes were deep and he seemed to be remembering just how bad things had been.

Then, without prompting, he said, "I'd hurt Mikayla's sister so Mikayla was mad at me herself. She let me know in no uncertain terms that I'd screwed up and she just couldn't let it go." Ry shook his head. "Poor Wyatt was stuck in the middle. Everything was…*bad*—awkward and uncomfortable and…bad. And because there *were* the family ties, there was no easy out. No way to make a clean break of things."

"I hadn't thought about that," Kate commiserated.

"Neither had I until a miserable Fourth of July party three months into the breakup. I thought everyone could just be cool about it if that was the tone I set. Paula was bringing someone, I wasn't, that seemed like a good way to just put everything behind us—"

"But you were wrong."

"Sooo wrong. It was ugly. I was dodging slings and arrows from Paula *and* from Mikayla the whole time. Then Paula caught me alone in the hallway, asked me if I was satisfied with the mess I'd made, and somehow that turned into her telling me she wanted to get back together. When I said that wouldn't work out, she went berserk again. Mikayla figured I'd provoked Paula, and…well, like I said, it was ugly."

He paused a moment as if to shake off the memory. Then he said, "It was enough to prove that while being with Mikayla was bad enough, there was no way Paula and I could be around each other. It was like a divorce, I guess. But that meant family occasions, dinners, events, holidays, had to be split up. For the two Thanksgivings after that, I planned ski trips and had to miss out so Paula could have Thanksgiving with Wyatt and Mikayla. I had those two Christmases with them while Paula went somewhere else, but Mikayla let me know she resented that I was there instead of her sister. It was lousy and by the time I went home after the second Christmas, I was figuring *all* of my holidays from then on were going to be spent alone."

"So if Wyatt's wife hadn't died—"

"Don't get me wrong—I would never say there was anything good about *that*. But yeah, if she hadn't died, things wouldn't have been the same for Wyatt and me. We would have gone on working together, but outside of work…that would have always been complicated."

Ry paused a moment and then, on a somewhat lighter note, he said, "Or maybe that's not true. Maybe I would have just had to wait a few more years. Because here you are, living in this small town with a guy who disappointed you. You must see each other almost every day, but you just said hello to him the same way you did to everyone else when we met up with him at Adz. I would have never known there had been anything between you if you hadn't told me. Did it just take longer for a truce to be called and the screaming, throwing-things part of the festivities to end?"

"I don't throw things," Kate said as if she was insulted that he should even suggest such a thing. "Or break windshields. And any screaming I *might* have done at Tommy was only at Tommy, in private, at the end of the relationship. Once it was over, that was it."

"There weren't any times when you provided a little local entertainment with a knock-down, drag-out fight during an accidental meeting at the ice cream parlor?"

Kate couldn't suppress a small smile at that idea. "I don't think my temperament is the same as what you've described of your former playmate or her sister. I'm not saying that there wasn't some awkwardness at first. But Tommy and I just avoided each other as much as we could. When we couldn't—because yes, this is a small town and we do share all the same friends—it wasn't as if we were warm and friendly. But we both opted for what you were going for at the Fourth of July party—we were civil and kept our distance."

Ry must have finally been convinced because he said, "Well then, my hat's off to you."

She'd rather have his shirt off, but she didn't say that. She just laughed. "Plus, in *my* family, emotional outbursts and displays of temper are a no-no."

"People can count on that with you?" he asked with what seemed like particular interest.

"Tantrums were never tolerated," Kate confirmed. "The Reverend wouldn't have it."

"I'm all in favor of not letting tempers flare," Ry said. Then he smiled that bad-boy smile as his focus seemed to shift, centering on her in a more concentrated way. "But the flaring of other things, that I'm all for."

"Such as?" she said, knowing that shift had suddenly taken them out of the unpleasant past and put them squarely back into the present.

"Such as…your excitement about flying yesterday for the first time—excitement is an emotional outburst that I'm all for. And you clocked me but good to get to that ball tonight—that kind of enthusiasm is pretty emotional stuff, but I'm all for that, too. And last night? Here on the couch?" His voice dropped an octave and he smiled a sexy, sexy smile. "That was a flare-up of the best kind. At least it was if it was coming from the *real* Kate Perry and not from the sake."

"I don't know, there was a *lot* of sake," Kate hedged. In retrospect, she knew full well that getting carried away the night before had only been about whatever it was that seemed to ignite between them when they were together. But she wasn't going to admit that.

"The sake, huh? That's a shame," he said, taking his hand from the sofa back to brush his knuckles along her cheek in the faintest of strokes. "Because more and more you make me think that not even the risk of far-reaching hell to pay is too high a price."

Kate couldn't help smiling at that. She liked the thought that he wanted her badly enough to be willing to take a risk. That was as exciting as flying.

"Then again, it might not have *only* been the sake," she said under her breath.

She didn't need to say more for him to grin. Or for him to slip his hand into the collar of the gauzy white shirt she was wearing over a tank top. He slid that hand to the back of her neck and pulled her forward just enough to meet him halfway when he leaned toward her to kiss her.

And even though a mere twenty-four hours had passed since the last time they'd kissed, Kate felt starved for it. For him. She felt as if being there alone with Ry again, kissing him, was exactly where she *should* be, where she should have been all along. Certainly it was where she *wanted* to be. And at that moment, that was all she thought.

That and how much she loved kissing him.

Why wouldn't she, though, when they'd gotten so good at it? When lips just seemed to know the exact moment to part. When tongues just seemed to know the exact moment to meet and where to take it from there.

Ry's other hand came to the side of her face and both of hers went to his chest, wishing yet again that that shirt would disappear.

But maybe she didn't have to just wish it.

She could take it off of him herself, couldn't she?

She could. But that would undoubtedly send a message and she knew that if she sent that message, she'd better mean it.

Just kiss him, she advised herself, and it was easy advice to take since kissing him *was* so nice.

One of Ry's arms wrapped around her to pull her nearer and Kate was only too willing to go, only too willing to have his hand find its way under her blouse, too, even if it was only in back and the tank top she had on still acted as a barrier between them.

It did give her another idea, though. She slipped her hands under the shirt she'd spent the last hour wanting off of him. At least she could feel what the shirt was covering. And feeling it was awfully nice, too.

He was all sleek skin over solid muscle and sinewy tendon, and Kate reveled in every inch of it, massaging it in a way that was completely sensual and visceral, and had absolutely nothing therapeutic to it.

His hand went from her neck into hair she'd left loose tonight, cupping her head as their kiss grew more intense. Then his other hand went from her back down her side, down her hip, to find her thigh where it was bare below the short, short cargo shorts she had on. And—like last night—he brought that leg over his so she could be closer still.

When she was, his hand didn't return to her back. Instead it went to her side again, under her shirt, making a slow climb to the outer edge of her breast—once more only on the outside of the tank top.

Kate could feel her pulse pick up speed anyway, her nipples tighten in anticipation and her breasts suddenly seemed to burgeon against the built-in bra of the tank top. She'd spent the whole night dying for his hands to be on her and now the possibility that it could happen again flooded her with an even worse craving for just that.

But she didn't get that craving met instantly. Ry paused. And if he was waiting to see if she was going to stop him, it was just a waste of time. Because there was nothing in Kate that wanted to stop him. She was just glad that he only used up a moment before he brought that hand around front.

Was it possible that it could feel even better tonight than it had last night? She didn't see how, and yet that was the way it seemed because as his hand enclosed her it felt so good a half sigh, half moan escaped her throat.

Then that big, strong hand at her breast began to make everything inside her rise to attention and with that their kiss kicked up a notch, too.

The tank top wasn't much interference and it easily gave way for Ry to reach beneath it to her naked skin, freeing her nipple to tighten and harden in his palm, making Kate almost purr with pleasure. She was sure that no massage of any kind could ever feel as wonderful as this did as he kneaded and caressed and stroked that pillow of flesh, as he circled and tugged and teased and tweaked the oh-so-alive crest.

His mouth left hers then, going to nibble on her ear, to dart a quick tongue into it, to nip the lobe before he kissed that spot just below it, just behind her jaw that he'd taught her was so sensitive, all the while keeping up the wonders he was working at her breasts.

He kissed and nudged the overblouse off one shoulder, taking the tank top's strap with it. Then he did the same thing on the other shoulder, freeing a path for kisses that brought his mouth to the uppermost curve of the breast his hand wasn't titillating.

Kate took a deep breath that made both breasts rise in encouragement. Encouragement he didn't seem to need as he went on kissing her all the way to the very tip where he took nipple and breast into the warm wetness of his mouth.

Kate swallowed back a very unladylike groan as his tongue flicked that taut kernel, as he sucked her deeply in.

Oh, what he was doing to her, and how it was making her want him.

The bed was right behind them in the studio apartment. It was laundry day. The sheets were clean. And the whole time she'd been changing them she'd been thinking about Ry. About last night. About what it might have been like if the evening had ended there rather than at the apartment's door.

Her hands were in his hair, holding his head to the magic he was making at her breast, her body was on fire with the need for more, and everything he was doing was only making that fire, that need, burn brighter.

But he isn't The One….

Did it matter?

Her body, her being, answered a resounding: *No! It doesn't matter!*

He rose up from her breast just then, and kissed her mouth again, sending his tongue on yet another adventure with hers while his hand went on tantalizing her breasts for a moment more. A moment that somehow seemed as if he were winding down when that was the last thing she had in mind.

But that was exactly what he was doing because then he took his hand from her breast, leaving the tank top in place again, and stopped kissing her.

"No sake tonight…" he said in explanation.

"No, no sake tonight."

"So you tell me—shall I stay or shall I go?"

And he'd even left her dressed enough to walk him to the door if that was the choice she made.

Kate kissed him, buying herself a minute that she didn't really need because she knew what she wanted. What she had to have.

He might not be The One, but he was the one she wanted right now. The one she couldn't deny herself. Not this time…

But he must have been determined to hear it for himself, because he ended that kiss, too, and repeated, "Shall I stay or shall I go?"

Tonight Kate did what he'd stopped her from doing the previous night—she moved her leg higher on his lap—and whispered, "Stay."

And that was when she saw the sexiest smile she'd ever seen from him. A moment before he kissed her again, a kiss that was so full of raw, hungry passion that it nearly took her breath away and made her wonder how he'd been containing so much until then.

That kiss was short, though. He ended it to turn off the table lamp, to stand, to take her hand and tug her to her feet, too.

He led her around the couch and up the single step that delineated her bedroom. And not once did Kate have a second thought about what she was going to do. She just couldn't wait to get where they were going so she could take that shirt off him!

Which was exactly what she did when they reached the side of her bed, feasting on the sight of that chest, those shoulders, those well-honed pectorals, as if he were a masterpiece. A masterpiece she could touch, and touch him she did—running her palms over every inch of that spectacular torso, ending at the waistband of his jeans.

He didn't wait for her to do what she was thinking about. He unfastened the button, unzipped the fly, dropped the jeans and the boxers with them.

And that was when the masterpiece was complete. Magnificent, in fact, as Kate stole a glance downward....

He didn't let her look for long, though, before he raised her chin with a hooked finger under it and kissed her again. Sweetly but not chastely, enticing her even more as he removed her clothes, too.

Naked in the moonlight coming through her open windows, Kate felt no shyness with him as he eased her onto the mattress and had a look of his own. A look that admired and adored and appreciated for just a moment before he lay down alongside her, running feather-light strokes of his fingertips from her shoulder, down her breast, down her side to her thigh. And then those fingertips came front and center.

He slipped his hand between her legs at the same time his mouth rediscovered first her mouth, then her breasts. And oh, the things he roused in her! Inhibitions evaporated and Kate reached for him, too, finding that long staff of steel that left no doubt that he wanted her as desperately as she wanted him.

She gave her all to exploring and learning and tormenting him, wanting to know him fully, wanting him to feel the same near-frenzy he was building in her.

And when that seemed to be just what she'd accomplished, he deserted her for a moment, reaching for their discarded clothes on the floor and returning with protection that he made quick work of using. Then he was back, kissing her once more as he rose above her, his hands on either side of her head.

Kate kissed him in eager response, opening more than her mouth to him. With care and concern for her, he found his way, slipping into her only slightly, easing out, slipping farther in, until he was home.

He gave her a moment, only flexing inside of her, pulsing like her own heartbeat, making her want him all the more before he finally dived in a bit deeper, then pulled out, then deeper still.

Kate's arms were around him, her hands pressed to the breadth of his back, while her hips kept pace, meeting and withdrawing in perfect unison. Slowly at first. Then faster. Then even faster, their mouths joining and parting, too, Ry's chest taunting her breasts with the same there-and-gone-again.

Deeper, faster, deeper, faster, every inch of her was in tune with him, with his body, with the chain reaction he was setting off in her.

Like a tiny glimmer, her climax began. A glimmer that grew bigger and brighter, bigger and hotter, bigger and bolder. Until it overtook her, so bright and hot and bold, so amazing, she wasn't sure she could bear it—or bear for it to ever end—as it flooded all through her and filled her with an ecstasy more incredible than anything she'd known was possible.

When it began to ebb she realized her spine had arched off the bed, that she was clinging to Ry as waves of that same ecstasy caught him in its grip and drove him into her so completely it was as if they'd fused.

Only after one final shudder did he begin his descent. With it, he eased Kate to relax back onto the mattress again, deflating onto her, letting some of his weight rest on her. And that was how they stayed for a long moment while they each caught their breath, while pounding hearts calmed, while the warm glow of aftermath wrapped around them.

"Wow…" Ry whispered into her ear then, awe echoing.

"Wow," she parroted with a smile, secretly relieved to know that she'd been able to wow him.

"Are you okay? I was a little out of control—I didn't hurt you or anything, did I?" he asked.

"No," she assured with an even bigger smile. "How about you? Did your shoulder hold up?"

"It could be broken and I wouldn't know the difference at this point," he said. But it must not have been any the worse for wear because he pushed himself up enough to look down at her as if he were seeing her through new eyes.

Then he kissed her again, a passionate, connecting kiss that let her know that he'd been as moved as she was.

Somewhere during that he rolled them to reverse their positions so that she was lying on top of him.

"I want to stay all night," he announced when the kiss that had gotten them there was over. "Can I?"

"I haven't posted any eviction notices, have I?" she responded, tightening her muscles around him since he was still inside of her.

He grinned a satisfied, replete grin and gently pressed her head to rest on his chest, cocooning her in his arms when he had. "You're full of surprises," he muttered in a voice that sounded thick and heavy with fatigue. "Can we take a catnap and then see what else might develop?"

Kate smiled, content to lie there with him as her mattress. "I guess we can see," she said as weariness overtook her, too.

He sighed then, a warm gust in her hair, and she knew he'd fallen asleep at precisely that moment.

But she didn't mind. She was just glad that he *was* staying.

Because if all she could have with him was this single night before she had to get back to reality and the goals she'd set for herself, she wanted as much of it—as much of him—as she could have.

Chapter Eleven

It was not often that Kate took a personal day. She had never—ever—taken one to spend the day in bed with a man.

But Monday—after a night that was heavy on lovemaking and very light on sleep—she had succumbed to Ry's persuasions and given herself an extension on that weekend that was supposed to have gotten him out of her system.

Breakfast in bed. Napping. Making love. Napping again. Making love again. Ry carrying her to the shower after playfully insisting that she overcome her own reservations and take one with him. Making love in the shower. Napping. Lunch in bed. Napping. Making love. Making love. Making love.

Apparently all that physical activity Ry enjoyed paid off in strength, resilience and stamina.

But by eight o'clock Monday evening they finally emerged from Kate's apartment. Ry was still determined to talk to Hector before the day was done, and Kate was hoping that some fresh air, and a taste of life and the world beyond Ry and her bed might help reinforce what she knew—that she had to put a stop to this weekend vacation from reality that she'd now added another day to.

Besides, she had more papers she needed to deliver to Hector and she thought that, if she did, she might feel a tiny bit less decadent and debauched about spending the last twenty-plus hours the way she had.

"Tyson *foreclosed* on somebody's farm?" Ry said as they went up the driveway after stopping at her office to get the papers and then driving to Hector Tyson's house.

"Hector bought the farm originally to flip it. Part of the deal he offered was to carry the loan when he sold it again. The Carsons bought it, but they haven't been able to make the farm earn what they needed for the payments and couldn't sell the place, so they defaulted," Kate explained. "Hector had the legal right, but it's been difficult for everyone to watch. At least the Carsons had somewhere to go—Kristy Carson's parents have a farm of their own a few miles farther out. They're letting Kristy and Michael move there with them."

"I haven't heard anything yet that makes me like this guy," Ry said after ringing Hector Tyson's doorbell. Then his expression softened as he looked down at her while they waited. "But you…you are an entirely different story."

Kate couldn't help smiling and being warmed by that.

"You doin' okay?" he said then, obviously delighting in the workout she'd sustained in their marathon of lovemaking.

"I don't think a very extended period of celibacy before last night was good training for what you did to me," she whispered.

"*What I did to you?* Hey, there were a few times that were *your* idea."

And the truth in that made her wonder how she was going to turn this all off now that she'd let it be turned on.

But the door opened just then and facing Hector Tyson suddenly took priority over everything else. For the time being, anyway.

"What did I tell you about bringing him around here, Kate?" Tyson demanded in greeting, staring daggers at Kate and refusing to look at Ry.

"She didn't have a choice," Ry answered before Kate could say anything. "She has papers for you and I have a deal to offer."

Hector's wrinkled face didn't change expressions but apparently Ry had sufficiently raised his interest because the old man stepped aside to let them in, not inviting them, merely allowing them entry.

Ry motioned for Kate to go in ahead of him, then followed behind.

Hector closed the door and again addressed Kate. "The papers on the Carson farm?"

Kate handed over the file she'd picked up from the office. "Your farm again now. These have been filed with the city and county," she said without inflection, accustomed to not showing Hector Tyson how much she disapproved of the things he did.

As always, the elderly man checked the paperwork, then set it on a nearby credenza before raising expectant, rheumy eyes to Ry.

"Let's go sit down," Ry suggested when it became clear that Hector had no intention of inviting them beyond the entryway.

Again Ry motioned for Kate to go first.

Kate looked from the grizzled Hector to the calm Ry, not sure what to do. But then Hector made the decision by ignoring Ry's courtesy to her and going into the living room himself, ahead of them both.

That just made Ry smile. "Come on," he encouraged Kate with a wink.

"My lawyer told me you've gone ahead with the lawsuit against me," Hector said when the three of them were sitting in the living room.

"We notified you that we intended to sue. The suit itself was the next step," Ry said logically.

"Two and a half million dollars!" Hector sneered. "You people are out of your minds."

The elderly man was sitting in a throne-like wing chair, stiff and imperial. Kate was perched at an angle on the edge of a sofa cushion so she could see both Hector and Ry— who was sitting casually beside her, his arms stretched wide along the back of the stuffy couch as if he didn't have a care in the world.

"Actually the two and a half million is lowball," he informed Hector matter-of-factly. "We might increase it once the audit of your personal and professional finances is finished and we learn exactly how much you benefited from selling the building materials for the houses that were built on the land. And in the meantime, our lawyers tell us we can turn your life upside down."

Kate had no idea if what Ry was saying was true. But Hector must have believed him because his bony cheeks took on an overly bright reddish color.

"What's the *deal* you have to offer?" the elderly man nearly growled in response.

"My grandmother doesn't care about you or your money," Ry said.

Kate couldn't be sure, but she thought she saw a muscle in Hector Tyson's face flinch, as if it might matter to him that Theresa didn't care anything about him. But it was there and gone in a split second and she thought she must have imagined it.

"The only thing my grandmother cares about," Ry continued, "is what happened to her baby—and don't bother denying that there *was* a baby because I have enough information outside of my grandmother's claim now to know that there was. Enough information to convince authorities."

Kate knew *that* was a bluff but there was such certainty in Ry's tone that there was no hint that he was lying.

"So here's the deal," Ry went on as if he were holding all the cards. "You can tell me what happened to the baby. That will make it quicker and easier for us, and save Gram any more anguish. As payment, my sister and brother and I have discussed it, and if you give us that information, we'll drop the lawsuit."

"If I refuse?" Hector asked.

Kate thought that it was like watching a poker game that had come down to two evenly matched players, and she wasn't sure which of them would win.

"If you refuse…" Ry mulled, smiling as though he would like to see Hector make that fool's move. "I'm going to take it as an admission that you did something worse than just find another home for the baby. Something you need to cover up, something you shouldn't have done and can't tell me without admitting to a crime and putting your ass in a ringer."

Hector grunted in a way that said that wasn't scaring him.

So Ry upped the ante. "At which point I'm not only going to the authorities with what I now know, I'll also use every connection my family has, every donation we've ever made to a political campaign, every favor and debt of gratitude owed to us, to make sure that while our lawyers are going after you in civil court, you're also being investigated to the hilt—"

"For some trumped-up—"

"For having made to disappear the infant that a teenage girl under your care, in your house, gave birth to. And I will feed the story to every newspaper, every magazine, every news station I can find to follow it. In short, Tyson, I have all the means to make your life miserable, and no qualms about using them."

"It was over fifty years ago!" Hector shouted.

"Actually, I'm told that with advancements in criminal investigation techniques—"

"There was no crime!" Hector finally said what his earlier grunt had only implied.

"Then save yourself a lot of grief and a huge amount of money, embarrassment and humiliation, and just tell me what I want to know," Ry advised.

If looks could kill, Hector Tyson's glare at Ry would have done it. His eyes were mere slits, his mouth was so puckered it looked like the top of a drawstring bag, and those red spots on his cheeks were the color of the town fire engine.

But Ry merely waited, unmoved by any of it.

Then Hector said, "Take Home-Max out of Northbridge, too."

Ry shook his head. "Home-Max stays. The only thing on the table is the lawsuit and the criminal investigation."

"There was no crime!" Hector repeated, louder still.

"Then there's no good reason not to tell us what we want to know. Especially since it's worth over two million dollars to you."

And yet Hector still had to consider it.

But after a few moments he slapped his hands on the arms of his chair in anger and said to Kate, "You're my witness—as the city clerk, you've heard him say the lawsuit will be dropped. That's a verbal agreement and legally binding."

"She's your witness," Ry agreed before Kate could say anything. "But let's hear it."

"The whole thing was for the best!" Hector insisted venomously. "Theresa knew that. She agreed with it."

"It was for the best that you take her baby away from her before she'd even laid eyes on it? Without so much as telling her whether it was a boy or a girl?" Ry said in disbelief.

"Theresa didn't want to see it or know anything about it if she had to give it up. She said it would be too hard, that she might not be able to. And it doesn't matter now, she's—the girl—is gone, she died in her twenties."

Kate glanced at Ry, watching his face sober before he said, "So the baby was a girl."

"A girl, yes."

"I'm not taking just your word for anything. I want the whole story, I want to know who she was, and how I find out for myself what happened to her," Ry said, setting the terms.

"Nothing is the way you think it was," Hector claimed, shaking his head at Ry. "Yes, I wanted Theresa's land. I had a right to it—I'd spent over a year working with her father on a plan for what to do with it. A plan I could still put into effect even though her father was dead. But not with a young girl as a partner. I only hoped to convince her to sell to me, that was all. The rest…"

Kate thought there was genuine regret in Hector Tyson's tone, in the second shake of his head.

"…the rest just happened. I know I was older. Nine years older. But I was barely twenty-six, she was seventeen—in those days any seventeen-year-old girl could have married a twenty-six-year-old man and there would have been nothing but celebration for a good match."

"Except that you were already married," Kate said, unable to refrain.

"To Grace. Who married me to spite a man who had jilted her. Who I married because her father made it financially worth my while." As if he'd said more than he wanted to on that subject, Hector shook it off and said, "Not that Grace wasn't a decent enough woman, she was. But there was never any affection between us."

"And then along came Theresa," Kate said, wanting to hear that he hadn't taken advantage of the young girl, that he'd cared about her.

"And then along came Theresa," Hector echoed with a slightly faraway note in his voice.

But it was there and gone a split second later when he said, "I'm not proud of what happened. But Theresa…she needed comforting and Grace didn't have it in her. It fell to me. I was Theresa's father's friend. I knew Theresa. It was me she came to when she was at her low points. Me she spent time with. And one thing just led to another…."

"You seduced her," Ry accused when the old man's mind seemed to wander.

"It wasn't like that. I'd found something with Theresa

that I'd never had before. But that didn't change that I was married to someone else."

Kate wondered if this was a performance that Hector was putting on, but she didn't see that there was anything for him to gain by confessing that he'd had feelings for Theresa, so she thought he was being honest.

"I ended things with Theresa almost as soon as they started," Hector went on defensively. "Before Grace even knew. But then we realized that there was going to be a baby. I told Theresa I would leave Grace, no matter how much it cost me. I was willing. It was what I wanted to do, and I know Theresa thought about it—"

"She also went to the minister and his wife about it," Ry said.

"And when she came back, she told me she wouldn't be the ruination of my marriage. Still, because of the baby, I had to tell Grace. If Grace had walked out herself…"

Kate thought that was what Hector had hoped for.

"But Grace didn't want that," he said with resignation. "She didn't want a divorce. She'd been shamed by one man leaving her, she wasn't going to let that happen again—"

"But there was still the baby," Ry reminded.

"Theresa knew she couldn't have it and raise it on her own—she wasn't strong or brave. Grace wouldn't hear of us keeping it, raising it as ours. Grace said that the baby needed to be given up completely—by me and by Theresa—given up and forgotten, so there would never be any bond between us. I told Theresa that and she agreed."

"Just like that?" Ry said skeptically, caustically.

"Not without tears and grief and depression and re-criminations and…no, not *just like that,*" Hector answered equally as caustically. "But it was what had to be done. For everyone's sake. Theresa agreed to hide the pregnancy, to give the baby up in secret once it was born, so no one would be the wiser. I promised her I would find it a good home, that then she could take the money for the land, leave town, and make a fresh start...."

"Who did you give the baby to?" Ry demanded, sounding unsympathetic to Hector and making Kate think that he didn't completely believe that Hector might have had an emotional attachment of his own to Theresa.

"There was a couple I knew who wanted a baby. They were desperate. But they didn't want it to be known that they couldn't have their own—Northbridge is a small, gossipy town, they didn't want to be the talk of it, they didn't want any child of theirs to forever be the *adopted* child. I made an arrangement with them. Anne claimed to be pregnant even though she wasn't. She padded her dresses, pretended. Theresa was grieving—it was easy to explain her staying away from her friends, not going out of the house much, wearing unbecoming clothes that hid things. And as soon as the baby was born—"

"You took it and passed it off to the other people," Ry finished for him.

"The next day Shamus made the announcement that they'd had their baby. A week later Theresa went to Missoula to live with her aunt. No one ever knew. No one was ever supposed to."

"Anne and Shamus?" Kate repeated. "The Wimmers?"

"Anne and Shamus Wimmer," Hector confirmed. "The child Theresa and I had was Maria Wimmer."

"And she married Frank McKendrick and had two children of her own. She died in childbirth," Kate filled in.

"You know these people?" Ry asked Kate.

"Logan and Hadley McKendrick—I grew up with them. They're your cousins. Theresa has two more grandchildren," Kate marveled.

But Ry was in a stare down with Hector by then. "Two grandchildren who are yours, too," he said to the old man.

"They don't know it," Hector answered gruffly but sounded genuinely saddened by that fact. "And I'm not so sure they'll be happy to find out."

Chapter Twelve

"Okay, how about if I go home, tell Gram what Tyson had to say, deal with whatever fallout *that* brings on, and then come back?"

Ry said that as Kate unlocked her apartment door and they were walking in. They'd just come from seeing Hector Tyson, from learning what Theresa Grayson had returned to her hometown to find out. Ry had wanted to go directly home, to take Kate with him to tell his grandmother the news. But Kate had insisted he bring her to her place instead.

When she turned on the end table lamp, she glanced up at the bed they'd made so much use of. It seemed to be calling to her, tempting her to make use of it again in that same way. All she would have to do was agree to what he was suggesting, assure him she would be waiting when he was finished giving his grandmother the news, that he could just come back and they could pick up where they'd left off.

It was so tempting.

But she knew the moment had arrived when she couldn't give in to that temptation.

Her two-day-stretched-to-three vacation from reality had to end. Her attraction to Ry hadn't been worked out of her system and she'd been telling herself during the entire drive from Hector's house that she couldn't let Ry be number four on the list of string-alongs that always cost her so dearly. That now was the time to take control of what was happening with him and stop it cold.

As much as she hated the idea.

And she hated it so much that it felt as if the sleeveless turtleneck she was wearing was choking her to keep her from saying what she knew she had to say.

But if she didn't do it now, if she waited for him to come back tonight, then what? Then they would go on seeing each other, and she would get in deeper and deeper while Ry would still leave the small town he was less-than-enchanted with and she'd be left waiting again. Waiting for the next time he came here. Waiting for him to play his sports or have his adventures or travel the world or keep himself stimulated in all those other ways that were what made him who he was. Waiting for him to want what she wanted, to be ready to settle down. Waiting patiently. Just like she'd waited for Tommy and Doug and T.C.

And she couldn't do that again. She wouldn't.

So she took a deep breath, tore her eyes—and her thoughts—away from the bed, and faced Ry, wishing that he wasn't the most gorgeous man she'd ever seen standing there big and tall in jeans and a bad-boy black T-shirt that caressed his body the way she wanted to.

She exhaled, tried to find some strength, and said, "The weekend is over."

Ry shrugged. "So?"

"So we have to stop...seeing...each other."

"Why?"

"I told you, Ry," she said as if this weren't coming out of the blue. "I know what I want, I'm going after it, and I won't be distracted again. I gave myself this weekend with you—this weekend that stretched into three days even though it shouldn't have. But now I can't let it go any longer than this. I can't let it interfere."

She stopped and shrugged as if it were just that simple when it felt anything but simple at all. Still, she wished he would say okay and leave. Leave her to deal with whatever fallout she was going to have to deal with in herself for this little fling she'd indulged in. This little fling that suddenly didn't seem like merely that, that suddenly seemed like a breakup that was going to be harder on her than all three of those others put together.

But Ry didn't say okay and leave. He didn't say anything for a long while, in fact. Long enough to make Kate uncomfortable as he stood there staring at her, his expression a kaleidoscope of emotions that she couldn't quite follow as she worked to hang on to her own resolve.

Then, when she began to wonder if he was ever going to say anything, he said, "What the hell, let's do it, Kate. Let's tie the knot."

"What?" Kate said in shock.

"Get hitched. Take the leap. You and me."

"Get *married? You're* crazy," was her response, not taking him seriously.

"I'm not crazy. I know that's what you want, what you should have, what you shouldn't have to wait any longer for. I know you're thinking that if I take up any more of your time, it'll just be more time wasted, and I don't want that for you. But I *do* want you."

"No," she answered as if it shouldn't need to be said. "That doesn't even make sense. We've only *known* each other a little more than a week."

"You're ready to pick a husband out of a catalog."

"Not a *husband,* a *potential* husband. Someone I won't spend a single minute with if he isn't looking for exactly the same thing I am. Someone I'll meet, date long enough to get to know, and then *maybe* pick as a husband," she amended.

"We've already met, dated, gotten to know each other. It doesn't matter that it was quick—things that are meant to be can happen that way. So pick me."

Despite the fact that he was being slightly flippant about it, Kate thought he actually meant what he was saying.

"*You* may do things without thinking, Ry, but—"

"But nothing. And this isn't something I'm doing without *thinking*—I was thinking about some of this this morning while I was watching you sleep."

Kate sighed. "I don't believe for a minute that you were thinking this morning about proposing."

"I was thinking about you. About how incredible you are. About how much more of you I wanted."

"*Wanted* in bed."

"Wanted in every way," he insisted firmly. "But now I'm here, after a week with you that's been a great week for no reason other than that I've been able to see you every day of it. I'm here after last night and today that were so damn amazing I'm still a little dazed. And it's just sinking in that that—oh, my God—you're trying to blow me off. And maybe that shouldn't be a big deal—I've been blown off before and it wasn't a big deal. Except that this *feels* like a big deal, and I don't want you to blow me off."

Okay, there was nothing flippant in that. But still, Kate said, "Ry—"

"No, don't *Ry* me," he ordered, going on. "I'm also picturing coming back to see my grandmother in a month or two months or six months and walking down that damn quaint small-town Main Street of yours and running into you. You, holding hands with some doofus you picked out of a catalog because his sole goal in life is to get married. And..." He shook his head. He shrugged. He sighed. "...and just imagining that is like I've been sucker punched. And something inside my head is screaming: *No! Don't let it happen! Don't let her blow you off! Don't let someone else have her!*"

"So it's a competitive thing," Kate said.

"No, it's not a competitive thing—I'm not Doug the dentist, and to me you aren't just some trophy I want to win over other guys. I told you even before this—I want to get married, to have kids—"

"*Someday,*" she reminded.

"Well, it turns out *someday* is today. And that you're who I want to do it all with."

"We aren't infatuated teenagers, Ry. You can't expect me to think anything but that you've lost your mind."

"Well, I haven't. Sometimes you just need to jump into the deep end—"

"I'm not the type who jumps into the deep end. I'm not *your* type, remember?" she said to reason with him.

"That's one of the things I was thinking about this morning—how mistaken I was at first, when I thought you weren't my type, when I thought you and I were so different, so wrong for each other. We aren't. We're really compatible. We're really right for each other because what makes us tick is pretty much the same, it just comes in the reverse order and that actually works for us—"

"I don't know what that means."

"It means that on the outside I'm the wild guy, I'm the risk-taker, I'm always up for fun and pushing the limits. That's the first thing anybody thinks when they think of me. But behind that, I'm all about coming back to home base, to my family. I've always done whatever it takes to stay close to Marti and Wyatt, to take care of Gram, because they're what matters most to me."

"I thought that because Tommy's friends and family were important to him that I would be, too, but that wasn't true."

"I'm telling you that *you and I* are alike, that I'm *not* like Doug the dentist or Tommy or that other guy, either. I'm not like any of the three selfish, self-centered jerks you've had in your life, no matter how it might look if you try to compare the obvious," Ry said, his voice louder. "I'm not *maturity-impaired* regardless of the things I do. Yes, I believe in squeezing every drop I can out of my life, but never at the expense of my responsibilities or my commitments or the people who are important to me. And I *keep* the commitments I make, I don't just make them and then put off following through. *That* was your trio of string-alongs. That isn't me. That isn't who *I* am even if that's what it looks like on the outside—which is part of my point."

He raised both hands to his head as if to keep frustration from making it explode. Then he dropped them to his hips, shifting his weight more to one than the other, and went on.

"What I was saying is that you and I are alike but in reverse order. Your outside just takes my inside to a greater extreme. You're the conservative Reverend's granddaughter who's all about family—your brothers and sister, your cousins, your mission to have a family of your own. Hell, I think Fiona and this whole town are just an extended family for you. But the importance of family isn't *different* from me, it's just up-front with you, and behind the scenes for me—the reverse order." He tilted his head and smiled an amused smile. "Then there's your inside…and now I know that you have a wild streak of your own—"

"I don't know anyone who would agree with that."

"I'm not saying it isn't well hidden. But it's there. I didn't think it was when I met you. When I met you I thought: wet blanket. And that night at Celeste's when Celeste and I were drinking ouzo and you turned up your nose at it? I was still thinking that you weren't for me. But now I know different. I know there's plenty of spirit behind the Reverend's granddaughter veneer. It's there in that toe ring you wear. It was there flying Saturday night and trying sushi and drinking too much sake. It was there when you were giving your all and clobbered me in that volleyball game. And in bed? It's not hidden there, that's for damn sure."

His smile became wicked, and Kate knew exactly what he was thinking about before he refocused, pressed a hand first to his chest and then gestured toward her. "My outside, your inside. Your outside, my inside. Reverse order," he repeated. "And yeah, it may take a little coaxing to get you to let loose, but it's worth it. And I like that I can be the one to do it. I like that it's not out there for everyone else. In fact, it's better that it's on the down low because Paula was actually too much like me and that doesn't work. But with you, there's just enough to keep me going, to keep me interested and challenged. And I think my coaxing keeps you from getting completely buried in the Reverend's grand-daughter bit. I think that if it isn't coaxed out every now and then, it will disappear. And that would be a shame."

He took a deep breath then, and said, "I think that what we have—what we are—together is the perfect balance. I think we complement each other. And you can't just blow that off."

Clearly he *had* given things between them some thought. A lot of thought. And it wasn't as if she disagreed with any of what he was saying, or that she didn't want to hang every hope she'd ever had on his words. But regard-less of how good he was at selling this, it wasn't anything she could go along with. Not even when she thought that, at that moment, he might believe that he wanted her to marry him. She could see how carried away he was. And no one thought rationally in that state of mind.

But she wasn't carried away. And she had to think ra-tionally.

And when she did, what she thought was that once Ry wasn't carried away, instant marriage was not going to be what he genuinely wanted.

"No, Ry," she said. "I can't believe we're even talking about this. It's silly."

"I'll tell you what *I* think is silly—that you made the decision that you have to get married and have kids ASAP, and now you're looking in a *catalog* for someone to plug into that decision. It's like you have the wedding arranged and you'll marry the first guy who fits into the tux—*that's* silly!"

"That isn't what I'm doing," she said, the analogy mak-ing her a little angry. "What I'm also not doing is marrying someone who wasn't even thinking about getting married or settling down an hour ago. Someone who probably won't still want to an hour from now. Someone who doesn't even take it seriously enough to actually use the right words. I'm not just looking in a *catalog* for a husband, I'm narrowing my search to men who have reached the same point in their lives that I've reached in mine—and not as a lark. Men who are ready to settle down, men who know without a doubt that they want to get married and have a family. Men who have made the same well-thought-out decision I have."

"That's the outside of you talking, Kate. The Reverend's conservative granddaughter. Don't let her be who decides this. Let the other part of you—"

"And then what? Then when you wake up tomorrow or a week from tomorrow or in a month or a year and realize you aren't any more ready than you were an hour ago, you put me off and put me off the way Tommy and Doug did? Or you panic like T.C. did?"

"I told you—"

"I know, not to compare you to them. But even if you aren't alike in other ways, you also aren't someone who's driven to put behind him whatever he has to in order to find a wife and start a family. That's where I am. That's what I want in the man I *plug into* the decision I've made. Because it all boils down to the same thing, Ry—*what the heck, let's do it, let's tie the knot* isn't a decision made after careful deliberation, after soul-searching and coming to the re-alization that that's truly the direction you want your life to go right now."

"Careful deliberation and soul-searching and coming to realizations may be how you reach decisions, Kate, but mine don't always have to be born of all that. Sometimes mine can spring to life at the spur of the moment and still be good decisions. That's part of what I was saying before—you and I can come at things differently but get to the same place. Allow for that. Accept that. Believe me when I tell you that I know myself well enough to be able to know what I want and what I'm doing *without* it always needing deep reflection and some kind of monumental revelation. Sometimes when it's right, you just know it. And that's how it is with this."

His energy and enthusiasm were infectious. And he *was* a master coaxer. And Kate was susceptible to it. To him. She wanted to let herself be swayed by him the way he'd persuaded her to do other things with him this week that she wouldn't have done otherwise.

But her wilder side wasn't her prevailing side. Her logical, conservative side was. And that side was making her shake her head no. It was forbidding her to let this go any further.

Before she could say that, though, Ry said, "Don't, Kate," as if he knew what she was about to do.

Then he closed the distance between them and took her by the arms, looking into her eyes so intently she thought he was trying to hypnotize her.

"You told me Saturday night that you wanted someone who would be as devoted to you as you would be to him," he said. "I can't stand the thought of you being devoted to anyone but me."

"Not being able to stand that thought isn't what's important here, Ry," Kate whispered.

"What do you think is more important to me at this minute than you are?" he demanded.

"We aren't talking about only this minute. We're talking about the rest of both our lives."

"I'm talking about *losing* what's most important to the rest of my life!" he shouted.

"No, you're talking about wanting something because you suddenly can't have it," she responded because that's what she was afraid this was about. And that the idea that he couldn't have her at all unless he married her had inspired his impetuous proposal. But in the end, if she gave him what he thought he wanted now, she would just be faced yet again with someone who wasn't ready to get married and so, ultimately, wouldn't.

"Come on," he cajoled. "Let go of the arguments you *can* make and just go with what's swept us along this whole last week—what's between us. Just go with that."

It was a nice thought. And it might have been the stuff fantasies were made of. But futures? Kate didn't think so. And she just couldn't risk ending up where she'd ended up before—disappointed and alone, with more time wasted—because Ry was venturing into this for reasons other than that this was what he really wanted.

"No," she said then. "I won't marry you just because marriage is what *I'm* looking for. I won't marry you because you don't want to be blown off. I won't marry you because you don't want me to marry anyone else, or because you've had a whim and you're used to following your whims. None of those are reasons to get married. So, no," she repeated, also very aware of the fact that nowhere in anything he'd said had he mentioned feelings beyond wanting her, either.

Ry shook his head this time, rejecting her refusal. "Marry me, Kate," he said, finally in the way it should have been said.

Her eyes filled with tears of sorrow, but she just took

another turn at that negative head shake, denying his request once more.

Then he surprised her by pulling her to him, kissing her so deeply, so thoroughly that it made her head spin.

And when it was over he repeated, "Marry me, Kate."

She knew what he was doing. He was trying to reach that less practical side of her that he was so good at bringing out.

But it didn't work.

Even weak-kneed and light-headed from that kiss, Kate's feet were still too firmly planted on the ground to waver. "No," she whispered definitively.

That made a muscle in his jaw pulse in a way she'd never seen before.

Then he let go of her, turned on his heels, and walked out of her apartment without another word.

And as a much heavier heartache than she'd anticipated took her in its grip, Kate tried to fight it off by thinking that even if she had said yes, they probably wouldn't have ended up at the altar anyway.

Chapter Thirteen

Ry's popularity in Northbridge didn't dwindle that next week and by the time Kate was trudging home from work on Friday evening she thought that if she had to hear his name one more time, she might pull her hair out.

She'd successfully avoided running into him, but hearing about him was something else. She'd listened endlessly to how he'd won this week's Bruisers baseball game by hitting four home runs. In celebration, the Bruisers had reportedly had a big barbecue the next night at a farm that belonged to another member of the team. According to the local chatter, Ry had wowed everyone with his dirt-bike skills and his willingness to bungee jump off a bridge on the property.

There had been an article in the town newspaper about how Ry was making unexpected headway with Home-Max. The store was now set to open ahead of schedule so hiring had begun.

And, of course, everyone was talking about how he'd solved the mystery of his grandmother's past, and how he and his siblings were ignoring the risk of more heirs staking a claim on what they'd built, and seeking out Theresa's other grandchildren so that Ry, Wyatt and Marti could meet them and arrange for them to meet Theresa.

Ry. Ry. Ry. He seemed to be the only thing anyone had talked about all week long. And since he'd also been the only thing Kate had been able to think about, trying to move on hadn't been aided by his name coming up every which way she'd turned.

To top it off Noah and Marti were back from their honeymoon. Kate had hoped that that would prompt Ry to return to Missoula. But it hadn't.

When she'd seen her brother and his new wife for lunch on Thursday, there wasn't any indication that they knew what had happened between her and Ry while they were gone and, as a result, they'd invited her to their own barbecue on Saturday night. Which they were happy to tell her Ry was also invited to.

The moment that invitation had been extended, Kate had recognized that Ry was right to have factored in that family connection when it came to their not getting involved with each other. Because she didn't know how she could possibly see him again and not crumble.

Since Tuesday, she'd done nothing but work, visit Fiona and seclude herself in her apartment where she'd spent most of her time crying and trying to figure out why the end of what had been nothing more than a few days of involvement had hit her this hard. Why every time she'd even tried to log on to the dating service sites or browse through the catalog from Partner-Finders, she'd ended up sobbing even harder on the bathroom floor instead of making any headway.

It had just been a little over a week with Ry! she kept shrieking at herself. *Nine* days! But it felt as if she'd lost someone who had been her whole world. There was just no way she could go out to her brother's ranch tomorrow night, put on a cheery face, and act as if nothing had happened.

Her feet were leaden as she climbed the steps to her apartment, still thinking about that barbecue. She'd decided that—even though she knew it would cause concern and questions and more attention than she wanted—she would call her brother and say she had the flu. It meant she'd have to hide out until Monday, but that's basically what she'd been doing all week anyway, and she'd arranged for someone else to visit Fiona, so she'd convinced herself that it wasn't doing any harm to lie. Then, once the barbecue was over, hopefully Ry would go back to Missoula, and by the time there was another family event that would bring her into contact with him, maybe she'd be on top of this thing.

That was her plan.

Not one she was proud of, but it would have to do.

There was an oversize manila envelope propped at her doorstep when she reached the landing. She was so mired in misery that she had almost no curiosity about what it could be. Barely glancing at it enough to notice that it was from Partner-Finders, she picked it up to take it inside.

"I can't even get through the first one and you're sending me a second?" she muttered, assuming by the size and weight of the package that it contained another catalog.

She was tempted to drop it—unopened—into the trash once she got it inside. But she'd paid a hefty amount of money to join all of the services she was supposed to be using to find herself a mate and she told herself that not only couldn't she let Ry—or any other not-ready-for-marriage man—waste her time, she shouldn't waste it herself. And if she was going to beg off her brother's dinner tomorrow night, her penance for the lie she intended to tell should be to force herself to look through the catalogs. And *not* compare any of the men in them to Ry.

Trying to summon some of the determination that she'd had before meeting Ry, she opened the envelope. What she found inside was, indeed, a catalog from Partner-Finders. The cover looked identical to the catalog she had, so she wondered if there had been some clerical error and she'd been sent a duplicate. If that was the case she would at least not be facing *two* catalogs to go through this weekend, so she opened it to see if the profiles inside seemed to be the same.

But inside were only a lot of blank pages and a single profile.

Of Ry Grayson.

She wasn't exactly sure why, but for the first time since he'd walked out of her door Monday night, she laughed.

"How did you pull this off?" she wondered out loud when closer inspection of the cover and the envelope made it apparent that it had genuinely come from the organization in Billings.

So what was he up to?

She'd had to dress for a city meeting this afternoon, which meant that she was in sandals and a sundress, her hair wound up into a bun at the back of her head. Craving comfort, she freed her hair, kicked off the sandals and took the catalog of one with her to sit on the sofa because she also hadn't had more than a few hours' sleep any night this week and she was weary.

From the couch, she propped her feet on the edge of the coffee table, set the binder on her lap and opened it. To a picture of Ry in grand and glorious living color.

The photographer had done him ample justice, capturing his charm, his mischievousness, his energy and spirit of adventure in that face the camera adored almost as much as Kate did. Even his metallic silver-blue eyes looked so vibrant and alive that they seemed to be staring at her, and it was almost as difficult for her to look at that picture of him as it would have been to meet him face-to-face this week.

Kate took a deep breath and forced her eyes off the photo, going on to read his profile instead.

The list of his interests was long and she was on it—in capital letters. He'd written that he was fun-loving and free-spirited on the outside, family-oriented on the inside. His greatest achievement was having met her. She was what he valued most. His goals and ambitions were to get married and have kids—with her. He'd listed her attributes—physical and otherwise—as what he was interested in.

And his one biggest regret was not telling her he loved her when he had had the chance.

"Oh, you're good," she moaned, feeling her heart twist and wanting to take this grand gesture seriously, pick up the phone and call him right that second.

But she didn't.

Because what this made her think was that, in rejecting him, she'd just made herself a greater challenge. And that now he was inclined to pull out all the stops. That's what Doug had done when she'd given him back his engagement ring. When it had been "too little, too late" with Doug.

Not that she didn't recognize that, on the whole, Ry genuinely *was* different than the three other men in her life—
the way he'd insisted.

In thinking about him almost every waking minute this
week, she'd had to admit that as she'd gotten to know Ry,
she hadn't found as much boy in him as she had in Tommy,
Doug and T.C. That while Ry's determination to live his
life to the fullest made some of his pursuits seem overly
youthful, when it came to the way he met his responsibilities to his family, to his grandmother, when she
factored in his work with underprivileged kids and his environmental concerns, it all tipped the scales away from
being maturity-impaired.

But nothing changed the fact that he also hadn't been
marriage-minded.

And now he wanted her to think he was.

"Well, he has had longer to consider it, after all," she
said facetiously, not actually believing that a few more
days mattered.

On the other hand, a little voice in the back of her mind
reasoned, he hadn't gone the way of T.C., either—apparently he didn't feel as if he'd dodged a bullet. Instead Ry
had obviously put time and thought and effort into trying
to get across to her that marriage was suddenly what he
actually did want.

Sooo…was it? that little voice pondered.

Kate went back to looking at his picture. At that face that
just made her melt.

Handsome and wild—that was Ry. But that wasn't *all*
he was. And now when she looked at him—even at merely
his photograph—in her mind she saw the man himself
three-dimensionally.

He might be a daredevil. He might be a thrill-seeker. But he also somehow managed not to be flighty. To be someone who did what he said he was going to do—which he'd proved in forcing the issue with Hector to help his grandmother.

He was someone who *was* devoted to his family, but who had also managed to juggle taking care of his grandmother last week, and doing his job and meeting his obligations to his siblings, with seeing Kate.

And he was someone who—despite a lengthy list of interests and pursuits—hadn't put a single thing before her.

No, on the whole, she admitted to herself, she thought Ry was one of the strongest, most stable, most well-rounded men she'd ever known—in spite of his outer, more reckless self.

And they *did* balance each other. Her reserve toned down his exuberance and seemed to have been a sort of respite that he'd liked escaping to when he'd had his fill of socializing and being the life of the party after each time they'd been out with everyone else.

And if she thought about being married to Ry, having kids with him? That balance they brought to each other, the way their reverse orders complemented each other, seemed like it just *might* make for the right blend.

But as she sat there still staring at Ry's picture she knew that no matter how laboriously she was reaching the same decision Ry had reached in a matter of minutes, the overwhelming reason for reaching it at all was because of how she felt about him. Because her feelings for him were bigger and stronger than anything she'd ever felt for a man. Deeper and more real.

"So I guess maybe you *are* The One, Ry Grayson," she told his picture. "And what am I going to do about it?"

"Look out your window?"

The sound of Ry's voice startled her into a gasp. Her head shot up and her eyes went instantly to the open window beside the apartment's door. Where Ry was coming up the stairs just outside and about to step onto the landing at that exact moment.

With the mock catalog still in hand, she met him at the door, opening it to let him in, and feeling her pulse pound at the fact that she was no longer looking at a picture of him, that she had the real thing right there before her.

But oddly enough, as they stood there facing each other just inside the door, the real thing looked as drawn as she felt, and more uncertain than she'd ever seen him.

"How did you do this?" she asked, motioning to the catalog as a jumble of thoughts crowded her mind.

He shrugged, a forlorn sort of frown continuing to mar his face. He crossed his arms over his dove-gray sport shirt in what almost looked like a protective gesture. "Money talks. And I had to join and promise that if I won you over I'd let them use us as a success story for their advertisements. But by now I thought Partner-Finders and I were both out of luck."

"By now?"

"I was hoping when it came yesterday that you wouldn't need a long time to think. I've been waiting and waiting and…to tell you the truth, until I heard you say what you just said, I thought…." He shrugged again. "I thought we were doomed."

"I didn't get this yesterday," she said. "It was waiting for me when I got home just now."

That seemed to cheer him up considerably. "It was supposed to come first thing yesterday morning. I've been thinking all this time that you must have looked at it and just thrown it out."

"Honestly, I only opened it now," Kate said, feeling some guilty pleasure at learning that he had apparently been suffering as much as she had been. Seeing for herself that losing her hadn't just been a small blip on his emotional radar helped her own sense that she was doing the right thing.

"But if you thought this hadn't worked, why are you here now?" she asked then.

"Marti invited me to her and Noah's barbecue tomorrow night and told me they're hoping you'll be there, too. I thought that even if you didn't want me, maybe we could talk about a plan for that." His smile then was the old, cocky Ry. "But if I'm *The One*..."

He took a step nearer, peering down at her still with a worried sort of intensity, but now with some intimacy sparking, too. "*Am* I The One?" he asked.

She could have pretended to play hard-to-get and maybe someone else might have. But she was just so glad that he was there, that there was hope for them, that she couldn't. "I know it took me a little longer to figure it out, but after doing some more thinking about everything, yeah, I think you are."

She went on to explain to him how she'd arrived at that decision, watching his handsome face finally let go of his own concerns by increments until she reached her conclusion and he was grinning.

"So basically you're telling me I was right," he goaded gently.

"I hope so," she said as a hint of her own misgivings crept in.

"No, no *hope so*," he corrected. "I was right—we are the perfect blend. It just took forever for you to make up your mind about it."

"Forever?" Kate repeated. "We still haven't even known each for a full two weeks."

"When lightning strikes…" he said as if that explained it. "But even if you *were* a little slow, at least you came around. By today, when I was never hearing from you and I thought I was done for, I wasn't sure how I was going to get by. I sure as hell didn't know how I was going to go to that barbecue tomorrow night and see you."

"You wouldn't have had to—I was going to fake the flu."

"The flu…" he said as if that gave him an idea. "You might be coming down with that anyway. We both might be."

"Why?"

"We *do* like to spend our weekends in bed, don't we?"

But that was apparently as much teasing as he was going to do for the moment because he closed the last distance that separated them, and when she looked up at him again, his expression was raw and open, and she could see that he genuinely had been feeling as bad as she had.

He took the catalog she still held and tossed it away. "I do love you, Kate," he said then, his voice quiet, as if what he was saying was coming straight from the heart. "I should have led with that Monday night."

He smiled sheepishly, reaching for her to pull her closer still, his arms draped loosely around her waist.

"But more than anything else," he went on, "that's why you knocked me for such a loop when you were ending things that I thought were just beginning. It's why I asked you to marry me."

Kate could see the pain she'd caused him and felt tears

fill her eyes. "I love you, too," she said for the first time. "And I'm sorry I misjudged you."

He smiled a small smile that said her apology was accepted and kissed her a tender, sweet, *hello* kind of kiss, tightening his arms around her.

When that kiss found a natural parting he looked at her, studying her face as if he couldn't get enough of it. "I was so afraid I was never going to have this again," said the man who never seemed afraid of anything.

Then he kissed her once more and began to show her what else he'd been afraid he might not have again as his hands massaged her back, caressing and kneading it, working the stress out of her to replace it with something much, much better.

Kate's hands found their way from pressing flat against his chest to unbuttoning his shirt. His found the zipper of her dress and eased it down. And while it didn't take long for clothes to be shed completely, for them to pull curtains and rediscover her bed, in all the times they'd made love that past weekend, this time was different.

Every kiss was savored, every touch, every texture, every moment—all of them cherished as if something precious had almost been lost.

But even though that was how it started, before long, intensity and hunger grew and engulfed them both.

Then urgency took over and the pure passion they'd shared that weekend before rose up to make each sensation sublime, each response a new reason to live.

Together they reconnected in an explosive pleasure so powerful that when it was reached, it held them both in its grip as if more than their bodies were melded, as if something deep within their souls, their spirits, fused in a way that nothing could ever drive apart.

And when it ended, it felt more like a new beginning as Kate lay in Ry's arms, her head pillowed by his shoulder.

"There's a problem, though," she said then, her voice raspy with passion. "I was going to make living in Northbridge one of my specifications for a mate."

Ry chuckled. "I know. I factored that in, too, on Monday when I proposed. I figured Marti and Wyatt and Gram will be here most of the time now—"

"Your grandmother!" Kate said with the reminder of Theresa. "I didn't even ask you how she's doing—Marti told me that it had been hard for her to find out that her daughter died, that she'd never be able to meet her."

"Yeah, Gram had some rough days right after I told her. Luckily I wasn't sleeping much myself, so I did the late nights with her. But she's coming around, I think. We keep reminding her that even though her daughter is gone, she has two more grandchildren. And we're trying to prepare her to meet them. And get in touch with them ourselves, too."

"So you'll have a lot of reasons to stay in Northbridge?" Kate asked, still hoping her hometown wasn't going to be too much of a sticking point.

"*You're* enough of a reason," he said. "But yeah, it looks like Northbridge has sucked me in. And even though this place has charm without a lot of action, I think I can fix that— I've been known to liven things up in the past, I'm pretty sure I can do it here, too. At least when I'm not busy peeling away your layers to get to that glimmer of wild streak in you."

"And kids?"

"Dozens, if that's what you want. As long as I can have you, and get you to live a little, I'm game for anything."

He craned his head up enough to kiss her again, a sexy kiss that might have started things all over again except that they were both exhausted from too many sleepless nights before this one.

Then he said, "I love you, Kate. And every minute of every day for the rest of my life I'm going to prove that to you. And I'm going to start with a wedding—any kind of wedding you want, anytime you say, the sooner the better, because I don't ever want to be without you again."

She smiled and kissed his chest. "You don't want to string me along?"

He trailed tantalizing fingers from her bare thigh, up her side, to a breast that he gave a squeeze before just hugging her tightly to him. "Only in the best ways and never without a big finish to make it worth it."

Kate laughed, raising her leg high up his thighs to do a little teasing of her own even though fatigue was weighing them both down and she knew this wasn't going anywhere until they'd had some sleep.

"You'd better rest up, then, because I'm going to hold you to that big-finish promise," she warned.

"Anytime, anyplace…" he said in a thick voice as he drifted off to sleep.

And as Kate finally found some rest of her own, she was thinking about Ry getting her to live a little.

She knew she would never live just a little with him. That her life with him would be much more than that. That it would be full and exciting and fun.

And better than she'd ever dreamed it would be.

Epilogue

Full hearts and too much excitement to keep contained were what pulled Kate and Ry out of their reunion bed late the following afternoon to go to Noah and Marti's barbecue after all.

But not without first stopping at the liquor store for Ry to buy a case of the best champagne the small town had to offer.

Popping the cork on the first bottle once they arrived at Kate's brother's ranch, Ry announced their engagement to the multitude of guests—most of whom Kate had known her entire life. Most of whom knew about her romantic failures.

But even though she braced herself for it, not once was there so much as a comment or a joke about whether or not she would make it to the altar this time.

Instead there were only well wishes, as if no one doubted that this would be the time that she did.

Then her brother Noah put it into words when he raised

his glass of champagne in toast and said, "To Ry and our Kate—who finally got it right!"

The cheers and applause that came in answer to that let Kate know that everyone really did give their stamp of approval to her fourth engagement.

And while she didn't need it, it was still nice to have it.

Nice to know that everyone realized what she'd realized—that, for her, Ry genuinely was The One.

The perfect one.

The one and only one.

The man she knew she actually would marry and spend the rest of her life with.

* * * * *

*Fan favorite Leslie Kelly is bringing her
readers a fantasy so scandalous,
we're calling it FORBIDDEN!*

*Look for
PLAY WITH ME
Available February 2010
from Harlequin® Blaze™.*

"AREN'T YOU GOING TO SAY 'Fly me' or at least 'Welcome aboard'?"

Amanda Bauer didn't. The softly muttered word that actually came out of her mouth was a lot less welcoming. And had fewer letters. Four, to be exact.

The man shook his head and tsked. "Not exactly the friendly skies. Haven't caught the spirit yet this morning?"

"Make one more airline-slogan crack and you'll be walking to Chicago," she said.

He nodded once, then pushed his sunglasses onto the top of his tousled hair. The move revealed blue eyes that matched the sky above. And yeah. They were twinkling. Damn it.

"Understood. Just, uh, promise me you'll say 'Coffee, tea or me' at least once, okay? Please?"

Amanda tried to glare, but that twinkle sucked the annoyance right out of her. She could only draw in a slow breath as he climbed into the plane. As she watched her passenger disappear into the small jet, she had to wonder about the trip she was about to take.

Coffee and tea they had, and he was welcome to them. But her? Well, she'd never even considered making a move on a customer before. Talk about unprofessional.

And yet...

Something inside her suddenly wanted to take a chance, to be a little outrageous.

How long since she had done indecent things—or decent ones, for that matter—with a sexy man? Not since before they'd thrown all their energies into expanding Clear-Blue Air, at the very least. She hadn't had time for a lunch date, much less the kind of lust-fest she'd enjoyed in her younger years. The kind that lasted for entire weekends and involved not leaving a bed except to grab the kind of sensuous food that could be smeared onto—and eaten off—someone else's hot, naked, sweat-tinged body.

She closed her eyes, her hand clenching tight on the railing. Her heart fluttered in her chest and she tried to make herself move. But she couldn't—not climbing up, but not backing away, either. Not physically, and not in her head.

Was she really considering this? God, she hadn't even looked at the stranger's left hand to make sure he was available. She had no idea if he was actually attracted to her or just an irrepressible flirt. Yet something inside was telling her to take a shot with this man.

It was crazy. Something she'd never considered. Yet right now, at this moment, she was definitely considering it. If he was available…could she do it? Seduce a stranger. Have an anonymous fling, like something out of a blue movie on late-night cable?

She didn't know. All she knew was that the flight to Chicago was a short one so she had to decide quickly. And as she put her foot on the bottom step and began to climb up, Amanda suddenly had to wonder if she was about to embark on the ride of her life.

*It all started
with a few naughty books....*

As a member of the Red Tote Book Club,
Carol Snow has been studying works of
classic erotic literature…but Carol doesn't
believe in love…or marriage. It's going to take
another kind of classic—Charles Dickens's
A Christmas Carol—and a little otherworldly
persuasion to convince her to go after her
own sexily ever after.

Cuddle up with

Her Sexy Valentine

by STEPHANIE BOND

Available February 2010

---

red-hot reads

Silhouette Desire

*Money can't buy him love…
but it can get his foot in the door*

He needed a wife…fast. And Texan Jeff Brand's
lovely new assistant would do just fine. After all,
the heat between him and Holly Lombard was
becoming impossible to resist. And a no-strings
marriage would certainly work for them both—
but will he be able to keep his feelings out of
this in-name-only union?

Find out in

MARRYING THE LONE STAR MAVERICK

by *USA TODAY* bestselling author
SARA ORWIG

Available in February

Always Powerful, Passionate and Provocative!

REQUEST YOUR FREE BOOKS!

2 FREE NOVELS PLUS 2 FREE GIFTS!

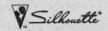

SPECIAL EDITION

Life, Love and Family!

HARLEQUIN
Ambassadors

Want to share your passion for reading Harlequin® Books?

Become a Harlequin Ambassador!

Harlequin Ambassadors are a group of passionate and well-connected readers who are willing to share their joy of reading Harlequin® books with family and friends.

You'll be sent all the tools you need to spark great conversation, including free books!

All we ask is that you share the romance with your friends and family!

You'll also be invited to have a say in new book ideas and exchange opinions with women just like you!

To see if you qualify* to be a Harlequin Ambassador, please visit
www.HarlequinAmbassadors.com.

*Please note that not everyone who applies to be a Harlequin Ambassador will qualify. For more information please visit www.HarlequinAmbassadors.com.

Thank you for your participation.

BAP09BPA